I0616704

DEADLY
Diva

K. P. HALL

Home & Leisure Publishing, Inc.
Lecanto, FL 34460

Published by
Home & Leisure Publishing, Inc.
P O Box 968
Lecanto, FL 34460-0968
www.halpi.com

First Printing, August 2010

Copyright © 1989 K. P. Hall

All rights reserved. This book, or parts thereof, may not be reproduced in
any form without permission; exceptions are made for brief excerpts used
in published reviews.

This is a work of fiction. Names, characters, places, or incidents are the
product of the author's imagination or used fictitiously and any
resemblence to actual persons, living or dead, events, or locales, is entirely
coincidental.

ISBN-10: 0-9825617-3-3
ISBN-13: 978-0-9825617-3-7

Printed in the United States of America

Being powerful is like being a lady. If you have to tell people you are, you aren't. — *Margaret Thatcher*

Last Words

She looked into the ornate bronze casket. Her father's face was serene, relaxed. She reached in, placed her hand on his, felt the waxy cold skin. There were muted whispers behind her, the old ladies weeping, her father's business partners murmuring.

"So devoted to each other."

"Sad, so sad. What a pity for her."

"She loved him so much. Such a tragedy."

The cloying smell of roses, carnations and mums began to overpower her and she gripped the edges of the casket as she started to swoon. Strong arms reached out to brace and steady her. She pulled free and bent down to the body within the casket, placed her mouth next to the waxy ear, felt the cold skin on her lips.

"You bastard, I should have killed you years ago," she whispered in her father's ear.

Marcella stood up and turned to return to her seat next to her husband. As she raised her head, she saw that Ed was looking toward the back of the church in Cissy's direction. A burst of black rage enveloped her.

As much as she detested funerals, Ed's might be next.

Luncheon With The Girls

"Young girls today don't seem to be doing any better than when I was growing up," said Karen as she reached for a hot croissant. "And, yet, they've certainly got a lot more advantages than my generation."

"Sounds like an 'I-had-to-walk-five-miles-in-the-snow-to-go-to-school' story," sneered Cissy.

"I'm talking about sex," Karen replied. "Your college major, remember?"

"What's the matter? Not getting any lately?" asked Cissy.

The five women were the only diners in the Garden Room. Their waiters, two this afternoon, remained a discreet distance away; the slightest movement in their direction brought them quickly to the table to pour more wine or refresh the glasses of chilled mineral water.

"Seriously, now—" Bobbi said.

"I take sex quite seriously," Cissy said.

"That's your problem," Marcella chimed in.

"Ah, lessons from the master."

"No, my dear, I leave that to you," Marcella retorted. She was very aware that Cissy was carrying Ed's child and she planned to make it impossible for Cissy to use her pregnancy as blackmail to get Ed away from her.

"Ladies," said Karen, "what I was trying to say is that back when most of us were feeling our first mating urges, if we'd had proper communication or some sort of decent training, be it at home or in the school system, it might have prepared us to properly deal with coming of age. Although with all the advances made in women's lib, young women today still seem to be making stupid mistakes when it comes to dealing with the sexual issue."

"So you'd have led your life differently if you'd been properly sex educated?" asked Candy.

"Possibly. Hopefully."

"For example?"

"Marcella, you grew up in the fifties. You remember how closed-mouthed everyone was when it came to talking about sex?" Karen looked at Marcella and waited for her nod of agreement.

"In my case, my mother was so inhibited about sex that when I turned fifteen she handed me a pamphlet with cartoon figures and told me to read it. That was my training about VD. When I asked her later just exactly how a person *got* VD she almost came apart with embarrassment. I dropped the subject with her. Besides which, my dance card wasn't exactly filled."

"My grandmother did much the same with me," responded Marcella. "We may have grown up in different decades, give or take a few years for some of us, but I don't think the age difference is that much of a factor."

"I'd personally like to drink a toast to Betty Friedan, Gloria Steinem and Hugh Hefner," said Bobbi raising her wine glass in a salute.

"I'll agree to that," said Karen returning the salute.

"Why Hugh Hefner?" asked Candy.

"Yeah, why Hugh Hefner?" Cissy sniggered. "Care to enlighten the babies of the crowd?"

"*Playboy Magazine* put photos of naked women within easy reach of pimply-faced young boys and it opened the way for the 'beaver shot' magazines that followed. Then Betty and Gloria came along and said, 'okay, girls, you've got their attention, so make yourselves heard as well as seen.' Betty told women they were entitled to orgasms. She refused to squeeze herself into the mold women had been forced to fit into for so many years," explained Karen.

"Doesn't sound so bad to me," said Candy.

"You wouldn't say that if that was your only option, believe me," responded Karen.

"So what would you have done differently, had you been more enlightened?" asked Bobbi.

"I probably wouldn't have married my first husband," replied Karen.

"Why?" asked Sandra.

"The honest truth is I married him because we had sex after we'd been dating for several months."

"You've got to be kidding!" snorted Cissy.

"No, I'm not," said Karen softly. "In the 1950's, my peer group didn't talk about sex when we got together so I had no earthly idea what the other girls were doing while I was trying to preserve my virginity. There were only two types of girls. Those who did-"

"And those who didn't," Marcella finished with a nod.

"So, in my case, when Tommy came along, and even though I knew he and I weren't a good match at all, there was a strong physical attraction I hadn't experienced before—"

"He bedded and you wedded," said Bobbi.

"In its simplest terms," said Karen.

"So how would Betty Friedan have saved you from such a fate?" asked Candy.

"She would have screwed him and moved on with no regrets."

"Succinctly put, Cissy," said Marcella. "Drawing from your personal credo, I presume?"

"Of course," replied Cissy with an icy smile.

"There's a lot to be said for promiscuity," Marcella responded.

"I think we're getting off track here," said Karen. "The point I wanted to make is that today's young women are lucky because they can make the same choices in their lifestyles that men have been allowed for centuries. Though I'm puzzled why so many of them are still falling into the old traps."

"But they still have to scratch and claw for their rightful place if you're talking about the business world," said Bobbi.

"That's true. Women's salaries remain well behind men's salaries for the same jobs," answered Karen. "And, unfortunately, even the EEO laws have been manipulated to put women in a very poor light in many instances. The government says put a woman in a high position, let's say vice president of a large corporation. Fine. The board of directors, all men, get together and pick their new female executive. The next thing you know she falls flat on her face and the men say 'see, we told you women just aren't equipped for such responsible business positions.' But the fact of the matter is, if women were chosen and groomed in the same manner in which men are women would be well equipped to handle any situation thrown at them."

"You're saying the deck is loaded against women in business?" asked Bobbi.

"You know it."

"Sure. As a matter of fact, I can give an example to back up what you've said. You remember my friend Juliann?"

"Yes," said Karen. "She got her MBA from Harvard, didn't she?"

"Yes. She was exceptionally qualified. Except at Harvard they didn't prepare her for the in-fighting and back stabbing in the real business world. So she accepted Dynatron Corporation's offer to be their vice president of marketing. That was her first mistake. She hadn't worked in the ranks long enough to learn their long range goals, find out their strengths and weaknesses, separate the good guys from the bad guys in the board room. She didn't know they were being been forced to put a woman in the board room to meet their EEO quota. She was a token female. No one expected her to succeed. And, once she was promoted, the wheels were put in motion to sabotage her at every turn."

"And?" asked Cissy.

"It worked. Sparing the gory details, she fell flat on her face within six months. The pity was, as qualified for the job as she was, she was naive and trusting enough to believe that everyone was on her side. She was given a choice, resign or be fired."

"I would have let them fire me," Candy said indignantly.

"She didn't. She resigned," said Bobbi.

"So she tucked her figurative tail between her legs and wimped off," said Sandra.

"Hardly. She started her own business. She took a few months to get her head together, evaluate what happened at Dynatron. When she finally realized how she'd been set up to fail she considered filing a discrimination suit. Before visiting a lawyer, she met with the board of directors and laid out the facts. She told me it was her pre-trial warm-up."

"So what happened?" asked Marcella.

"Well, Dynatron was up for a very juicy government contract and they didn't need any adverse publicity. They settled quietly, gentlemanly."

"How gentlemanly?" asked Cissy.

"A quarter million."

"Holy geez!" yelped Candy.

"And that government contract? Dynatron's bid was not quite as good as one from an upstart minority-owned company. Did you know that women business owners are considered minorities? That contract was the first of many that went to Juliann, not Dynatron."

"She went into business against them?"

"Sure. She did her homework, found their weaknesses and capitalized on them. Her corporation's on the big board now, trading a few points higher than Dynatron, and still climbing."

"I'll bet they're pissed," said Candy.

"That's putting it mildly. They offered to buy her corporation. She refused. They suggested a merger. She refused. She says she's going to bury them."

"I thought you said she was naive," said Karen.

"Naive, yes, but not a slow learner."

Marcella sat back and smiled. They were an incongruous group but she needed each of them.

She considered Karen Bryce to be her closest friend and confidant or at least as much of a confidant as she needed when it suited her. Karen had a middle-class background, climbed the corporate ladder by hard work and perseverance, and when she divorced her first husband, she dove headlong into a pursuit of the arts.

Marcella met Karen at an arts festival and found they shared a common ground: they were both mediocre watercolorists. When Karen's second husband, a wealthy importer-exporter, died from a massive stroke, she continued to indulge her passion for art by collecting great works instead of attempting to paint them.

Bobbi Adams was best described as the adventuresome type. She and her boyfriend, Chris Ward, spent their leisure time traveling, mountain climbing, cave diving, parachute jumping, or pursuing other unusual and/or dangerous activities. They each had significant earnings from inherited monies which were invested in blue chip stocks and they could easily travel the world and indulge their whims without care.

Bobbi and Chris also possessed a deep love and appreciation of nature and volunteered their time plus considerable amounts of money for several of Marcella's environmental projects.

Bobbi, in her late thirties, was attractive in a rugged way, with short cropped blonde hair, a medium complexion, dark hazel eyes and high cheekbones. She was a no-nonsense person who didn't accept flattery well and who despised shallowness in people, which was the reason she was not pleased to be sitting at the same table with Sandra Bianci.

There weren't too many women in Tampa society who liked Herbert Bianci's young wife, most considering her to be a conniving gold-digger who latched onto a lonely old man for his money and social status. That she had removed an eligible man from their midst —whether for themselves or their socialite daughters — was a consideration conspicuously ignored.

Sandra tried to fit into the social scene without having an understanding of the rules of the game. She played the part of the wealthy society matron and doled out party invitations to a select few in order to have an audience to showcase her imported designer gowns and extravagant jewelry collection. Those who accepted her invitations did so out of respect for her husband, his standing in the community, his business clout, not out of a liking for her. Sandra's parties did, however, provide fodder for the gossip mills and the society matrons were constantly tittering over her latest gaucheries.

Marcella felt pity for the girl since it was evident she didn't come from a monied background nor was she a scholar either by formal education or natural ability, although she displayed an animal instinct for survival. Because Herbert was a lifelong friend, Marcella included Sandra in the majority of her functions. Marcella also wanted to keep a close watch over Sandra's activities. She, too, had been outraged when Herbert returned from a gambling junket with his new young wife in tow.

Cissy Turlington was a dramatic looking woman who dressed impeccably, wore huge solitaire diamonds on her well-manicured fingers, had sleek short black hair that hugged her head, and gold-flecked dark grey eyes that were striking in their intensity.

Cissy had been Ed's secretary. She then became his mistress. Ed always had a mistress, sometimes two or three at the same time, but Cissy was different. Marcella learned the full extent of Cissy's control over Ed when he promoted her to operations manager of Grand Enterprises, the shipbuilding company Marcella inherited from her father.

Marcella masked her loathing for Cissy so she could better keep an eye on her. She included Cissy in her various functions and Cissy attended them all for she knew each was a steppingstone to where she aspired to be — in Marcella's shoes.

Candy Jones, a voluptuous young blonde with previous work experience as an executive secretary in various corporations was employed as Marcella's social secretary. Candy was a docile creature who made men drool and most women want to mother her.

Marcella knew of Candy's comprehensive sexual history, her willingness to please and her inability to say no. Candy was charming, pleasant, not overly ambitious, and able to cajole just about anyone into just about anything.

Marcella made it clear from the start that Candy's personal life was to be kept separate from her obligations to Marcella. Candy readily agreed. Marcella paid her a hefty salary, let her drive the red Mercedes SL coupe, took her on business and pleasure trips to exotic countries, and taught her the secret of "the big O."

Candy became Marcella's eyes and ears and her affable manner made her the perfect shoulder to cry on as well as a good listening post. Candy was the one who kept Marcella up-to-date about Ed and Cissy's long affair, getting information directly from Cissy.

Candy and Cissy attended the same health spa and it was easy for Cissy to confide in the dumb blonde with the big boobs. While Cissy regarded Candy with contempt, she had no one else to talk with. Cissy had no clue Candy had a memory for detail and a loathing for her that almost matched Marcella's.

"Children," said Marcella as she waved for the check. "All this talk about women's equality and sex has worn me out. It's time for this old lady to go home for her afternoon nap."

Karen and Bobbi broke into gales of laughter.

"I said something amusing?" asked Marcella.

"You don't take afternoon naps," said Karen.

"How do you know?" asked Marcella testily.

"Because you have appointments set with every state environmental agency from now until a year from now for all I know. You don't take nap breaks. That I know," replied Karen.

"Yeah, work, work, work, that's your motto, Marcella," agreed Bobbi.

Marcella smiled. They thought they knew her so well, yet they didn't know her at all.

"You never finished telling us why you wouldn't have married Tommy," said Candy.

"Oh, I don't think you want to know all the details. And, besides, Marcella needs her rest," said Karen. The truth was she preferred to keep her private life just that.

"I think I can stay awake a bit longer," said Marcella with a smile.

"Really, I'd like to know," Candy prompted.

"Me, too," agreed Sandra.

"Might be interesting, though I doubt it," Cissy responded.

"Karen, you said you came from a different decade. Care to elaborate without making yourself out to be too ancient?" asked Bobbi.

"Just a little. Marcella, promise you'll stop me if I go over three minutes' worth of life story. Okay?"

Marcella nodded.

"First, I grew up with Howdy Doody, Buffalo Bob, Father Knows Best, Ozzie and Harriett, Ed Sullivan. Real 1950's bland, everything pure and naive."

"Howdy Doody? Never heard of him," said Sandra.

"A bit before your time," said Marcella.

"Before mine, too," Candy chimed in.

"And me," snickered Cissy.

Marcella shot a black look at Cissy. "Don't push it," she cautioned.

"As I was saying, I grew up in a time when people just didn't acknowledge that sex existed. Honest to God, I didn't know about penises or vaginas. I certainly didn't know it took one inside the other to make babies."

"You're kidding, right?" Cissy snorted.

"No. And I was no raving beauty so I didn't have the boys lined up waiting to show me theirs if I'd show them mine."

"So how did you meet Tommy? Didn't you say he was quite a lady killer? You don't sound like you were his type," asked Sandra. She wanted to draw Karen's story out as long as possible, afraid if there was a lull it would be her turn.

"It was my car."

"A car?" asked Candy. "Maybe I've been using the wrong approach all these years."

"My fantasy car, a white 1958 T-bird convertible."

"I bought one for Ed just after we got married," said Marcella. "My mistake."

Cissy raised her eyebrows.

"Turned into a pussy catcher," Marcella said spitting the words out.

"Marcella! You shock me!" chortled Karen.

"You know what I mean," said Marcella.

"Sure do. Anyway, just after I got my little sports car, Tommy saw me driving it and thought I had to be as hot as my car. What a surprise he got. He figured I was another one of his usual hit and run floozy types. To make a very long and boring story as short as possible, we dated steadily, Tommy's version of steadily, for over two years."

"His version?" asked Candy.

"Same as the married man who responds to the question of whether he's married, 'no, but my wife is.' I went steady and he dated every cocktail waitress in town."

"Seems reasonable if you were as naive as you say you were," said Cissy.

"I was in the beginning. He gave me a fairly complete introduction into what pleased him, despite my pleas of innocence. Shocked the heck out of him when he discovered I truly was the virgin I claimed to be."

"Can a man really tell?" asked Candy.

"No, that's a bunch of crap!" declared Cissy.

"Beats me, but I don't think so," said Karen. "Anyway, he was one of those old-fashioned types who bangs everything in skirts but will only marry a virgin. There are still some around, but I think it's safe to say times are changing to more equality with guys wanting their future wives to be more skilled between the sheets. Suffice it to say that when we finally did get married, and it was all because I pushed it, not him, we didn't have the most honest relationship."

"Other women?" asked Marcella as she looked at Cissy.

"Yep."

"Didn't you ever cheat?" asked Sandra.

"No."

"Not even one time? Didn't you even want to?" asked Sandra.

"Not really. I truly, in my own sheltered way, loved the guy. And, I was scared of him."

"Scared? Why?" prompted Candy.

"He was fanatically jealous without reason. Or maybe it was projection since he was a serial cheater throughout our marriage. He threatened to kill me if he ever caught me with anyone else. If I went to the grocery store and was gone two minutes longer than he determined I should be, I had to be with my lover. Finally, I outgrew him and left. Period. End of story."

"Doesn't sound like the end to me," said Cissy.

"Your three minutes are up," Marcella said to Karen. "I think it's time to get a younger woman's story for contrast. How about it, Candy? Sandra?"

"I may be younger than Karen but as a teenager I think we probably were equals as far as innocence goes," replied Candy.

"Give me a break!" Cissy snorted. "You?!"

"Me. I led such a sheltered life I actually thought I'd been raped when a guy Frenched me."

"You have to be kidding! So what got your sex machine running? You sure aren't the starry-eyed virgin now," said Cissy.

"Books," replied Candy.

"Books?" echoed Sandra.

"Books. I started reading some real erotic stuff, at least it was for ten years ago. You know, *Joy of Sex*, with those nice graphic pictures. Lots of others."

"Hey! Are you daydreaming?" Marcella cut into Karen's thoughts.

"Ummm?" asked Karen.

"I certainly hope you've been listening," said Marcella.

"Of course," said Karen. "If Candy tells us any more of her x-rated life story, we're going to be barred from this restaurant."

Candy blushed while the others laughed. It was good-natured ribbing, for the most part.

"Ladies, I really do need to get going," said Marcella as she rose from her chair.

"I love our conversations!" Candy enthused.

"You would," said Cissy. "Frankly, I think they're a waste of my time."

"No one's holding a gun to your head to make you attend," said Bobbi.

"Yeah, sure. I already know how it works with a bunch of women. The one who doesn't show is that day's topic of conversation."

"Why, Cissy, what *ever* would we find interesting enough about you to talk about?" Candy asked.

"Ladies, you should have all received your invitations to my party next week. Until then," said Marcella as she walked toward the door.

Marcella

Marcella was a striking woman for her age. Her strong features and distinctive fashion style worked well with her bone structure. Her olive complexion, thick dark hair and vibrant brown eyes made her appear younger than her age of fifty-five.

Marcella was the first person to volunteer for any worthy (and sometimes not so worthy) cause, be it obtaining funding for the new arts center, recruiting pink ladies for hospital work, or fighting environmental degradation. She was a tireless worker who enjoyed the accolades she garnered by her accomplishments.

There was more to Marcella's generous volunteering than a simple love for humanity. Years of intensive therapy taught her how to mask dark violence with a gregarious persona. Under the poised, take-charge exterior was a terrible child filled with black rage, a child capable of monstrous deeds.

Marcella basked in the glow of work well done, accomplishments completed. As a woman full of self-doubt about her own worth, she needed to be the most visible benefactor of the arts, the loudest environmental watchdog, the one person who could be counted upon — no matter how demanding the cause — to plunge headlong into any and every project. Her self-worth grew as she was toasted, courted and praised by her peers and the media.

She drove herself maniacally in an attempt to block out the knowledge of her husband's sexual exploits. Ed had been Marcella's only love and his erotic appetite was a festering wound. The pity of her friends served to anger her more.

Marcella's grandparents immigrated from Cuba and settled in Ybor City, the Cuban section of Tampa. They had little money, but for the hard working immigrants money was not as important, nor as valuable, as freedom.

Arturo Granda, Marcella's grandfather, worked in a cigar factory. He was hired as a roller then promoted to roller foreman. Because he was an honest, hard-working employee, he was given more responsibility which meant more money for his family. The additional money was sorely needed inasmuch as the family had grown since the couple's arrival in the United States eleven years before. There was ten-year-old

Manuel, eight-year-old Santos, five-year-old Maria, and three-year-old Carlos. Despite the costs involved in raising such a large family, Mama Marcella pinched pennies, stretched dollars and was always able to put a little something away "for a rainy day."

Their savings were put to good use when Arturo was offered a partnership in the cigar factory. Business had not been as profitable as the owners expected and they needed additional capital. Believing Arturo to be a less than brilliant businessman, they offered him a portion of the business in exchange for his savings. What they hadn't counted on was Arturo's capacity for understanding accounting ledgers. He soon uncovered losses due to the ineptness of the elderly bookkeeper, who was promptly retired.

Once Arturo had the books in good repair he set about refining the operation of the factory and improving employee morale by upgrading working conditions. A reader was employed to read the daily newspaper and popular books to the workers as they sat at the long tables wrapping fragrant tobacco leaves around the specially blended core. With better working conditions, production increased and the business began showing substantial profits.

Mama Marcella continued to pinch and stretch the money Arturo brought home. Carlos was a sickly youngster who spent much of his childhood being doctored for a variety of ills. While Carlos' medications took a substantial bite out of the family's savings, the money that did reach the bank steadily grew.

Because he kept reinvesting, by the time World War I began, Arturo owned virtually all stock in the cigar factory.

Arturo's age prevented him from going to war. Manuel and Santos raced to join the army to defend their beloved United States and both lost their lives, earning posthumous Purple Hearts. Carlos, not particularly eager to follow his brothers into war, was rejected because of his health history.

Maria married her childhood sweetheart before he left for the war, and was a victim of the great influenza epidemic that swept through Tampa in 1918.

And so it was that the Granda family had one child to pass on the name and the bloodline. Carlos was perhaps not the best choice, but he was the only child remaining.

Mama Marcella pampered Carlos despite Arturo's warnings that he needed a firm hand to guide him. Carlos knew how to maneuver his mother to his wishes and he knew how to avoid direct confrontations with his strong-willed father. He glided through the war years clothed in the finest fashions, pockets filled with spending money Mama Marcella pulled from savings. She lost much of her zest for life with the death of her three older children and lived only to provide Carlos with everything she would never have a chance to give to Maria, Santos or Manuel.

Carlos was a product of his indulgent mother, playing fast and loose, spending his parents' money on fancy clothes, fast cars and loose women. His father attempted to involve him in the operations of the cigar factory, intending to groom him as his successor but Carlos had no interest in the factory and preferred to play. The flow of money from his mother continued.

After Arturo Granda's heart exploded while he celebrated at Ybor City's New Year's gala of 1928, Carlos had little choice but to learn the cigar business, and quickly. Like his father, he had a natural affinity for business management and he was able to cut back and hold onto the factory when the market fell in 1929. While most of their friends and business acquaintances were selling their fine art, jewelry, and big homes during the early 1930's, Carlos and his mother continued along with their same lifestyle, albeit a bit on the conservative side from Carlos' vantage point.

Carlos, having always considered the cigar factory a mid-point to success, took advantage of poor management practices by his friend John Arnett and purchased Arnett's failing shipyard with monies from the sale of the cigar factory to his major competitor.

Carlos then anglicized his name to Carl Grand, much to his mother's dismay. As Carl Grand, wealthy shipyard owner, he continued to cut a wide path through the available women of Tampa, ignoring his mother's pleas to marry and give her many grand-children. Marriage didn't fit into his plans.

Carl had not anticipated falling in love with Anna Busciglio, the fiery 18-year-old who captivated the handsome 37-year-old bachelor with her dancing eyes and supple young body.

Anna and Carl were married within two months of their first meeting and moved into the Granda family home, the huge Hyde Park mansion Arturo Granda designed and built at the turn of the century. Mama Marcella was delighted.

Anna was an enchanting young girl and Mama Marcella took under her tutelage, teaching her the proper preparation of Carlos' favorite foods, arroz con pollo, black beans and rice, boliche, rich pastries, thick coffee con leche.

Carl and Anna were ecstatically, breathlessly in love. It was the power of first love for Carl after years of frivolous affairs. It was the magnitude of virginal love for Anna.

There was cause for celebration in the Granda and Busciglio families when, after six months of blissful marriage, Anna became pregnant.

Carl and Anna's baby girl was born on Friday, September 13, 1935. And, on that date, Anna died from the complications of childbirth.

Carl, grief-stricken, mourned the death of his young wife and turned his back on his newborn daughter, wishing he was burying the child instead of his beautiful Anna.

Carl moved out of the Hyde Park house, leaving his infant daughter for his mother to raise. He provided money for their needs but refused to visit the child. He returned to his earlier ways and used and discarded women with great abandon. He was even more sought after by the foolish women who now pressed him to their bosoms in attempts to comfort and offer him solace.

Carlos' mother had his child christened using the name chosen by Anna: Marcella Anna.

As young children are apt to do, Marcella Anna had pretend friends who took the place, as best as pretend friends can, of her absentee father.

The teenaged Marcella Anna outwardly accepted her father's rejection, although she attempted to get his attention first through academic accomplishments, and, when that didn't work, through outrageous behavior, which only served to upset her grandmother whom she loved dearly.

As a small child, Marcella Anna displayed sporadic outbreaks of anger, mostly directed toward her absentee father. Because her fits were so violent and upset her grandmother, she learned to hide her rage. As she grew older, her anger festered into a black rage.

There were days when she considered putting a bullet through her brain but it was the raging child that controlled the violent woman, exacting revenge on those she saw as a threat.

The humiliation of Ed's flagrant sexual escapades was almost more than Marcella could handle, but she knew that if she acknowledged his cheating she would be forced to take action to save face. She turned a deaf ear to the busybodies who, in her own best interest, naturally, kept her apprised of Ed's philandering. She thought bitterly that they should watch their own husbands instead, since Ed wasn't the only cheater within their social circle.

Marcella used Candy as her confidant and spy who dutifully told her names, dates and places of Ed's trysts. Marcella recognized she held the position of strength as long as she knew and used that knowledge to make her own decisions about her life.

Long ago Marcella had chosen to remain in a faithless marriage rather than lose the public and social security a husband provided. She knew, too, that Ed didn't want a divorce. There were too many bimbos to whom he'd promised marriage in order to prolong a relationship, using Marcella's refusal of a divorce as the silver thread to maintain, or, if need be, discard a lover. She despised her husband as intensely as she had despised her father. But she used her husband as she had eventually learned to use her father.

When Marcella was a young child, her father, feeling a small measure of guilt over his rejection of her, gave her money and expensive gifts. But he very rarely visited, and it was always her grandmother who was in the audience at school functions, including her high school and college graduations.

When her father had a new Corvette convertible delivered to her the afternoon of her high school graduation, Marcella made the salesman park it in the garage where it stayed, untouched, for four months while Marcella continued to drive the worn out Kaiser her grandmother helped her buy the year before.

When she'd been a very little girl, Marcella asked her grandmother questions about her parents. Her grandmother had shown her pictures of the young couple taken on their honeymoon and it was evident they were very much in love. Marcella kept the pictures in her nightstand next to her bed and occasionally took them out to study the happy faces.

Her father was a tall, lean, handsome man who vaguely resembled the photographs in her nightstand.

But he was older, and his thick black hair was laced with gray, and he had cold bitter eyes. He rarely smiled, and when he did, it was for his mother, never for Marcella. For her he was reserved, withdrawn.

As she grew older she continued to compare the beautiful young woman in the photographs with the reflection in her mirror. The woman in the photographs was petite with dark hair that cascaded over her shoulders. The young woman in the photographs was beautiful and vibrant, with sparkling eyes and full sensuous lips.

The reflection in Marcella's mirror was all wrong. She wanted to see the same image as in the photographs, but she didn't. Instead, she saw a raw-boned body topped by a strong-featured face. She was big-boned, sturdy.

Years of comforting herself with large helpings of her grandmother's cooking added unattractive layers of fat to her large frame. Her indulgence in sweets hadn't helped her complexion, intensifying an adolescent acne problem. Her coarse black hair proved to be unmanageable so she pulled it back from her face, and secured it in a tight roll at the nape of her neck.

No, she wasn't her mother's child, and for that she was angry. Perhaps, she reasoned, she could have gotten her father's love if she had some of her mother's features.

Marcella knew her father was wealthy, the major portion of his wealth made during World War II when the shipyards were active 24-hours a day, seven days a week. Carl Grand had been too old to be drafted, and he presented papers showing he had sole responsibility for a child as well as his elderly mother.

His business was crucial to the war effort but the majority of his workers were young men who went off to war. He put together a new work force of men too old to go to war, and the wives and sisters of his drafted employees.

The war was good for Carl Grand, increasing his wealth many times over, making him a very powerful man in Tampa society. It also made his daughter a desirable catch in the eyes of the society matrons, though not in their young sons' eyes since the wealthy young men preferred lush, tender, doe-eyed debs.

Marcella received an early introduction to the sex act having allowed a brash young classmate to deflower her when she was fourteen. She found nothing pleasurable about the act and it was the only sexual intimacy she had ever allowed. Not that she was besieged with dates — she wasn't.

It was her grandmother who arranged for an escort to take her to her high school senior prom and the boy was less than enthusiastic throughout the activities, paying a minimal amount of attention to her.

Marcella commuted to the local university instead of going to a more prestigious institution. She had no driving need to become more literate, believing she would always be shunned and overlooked, that brains were no substitute for beauty. Later she would learn that wealth was the great equalizer.

It was at the university, as she plodded through her biology and anthropology courses, devouring textbooks by the score, that she discovered a hidden love for nature in all its forms. She excelled in science, biology, zoology. Her professors praised her lavishly, and Marcella, for the first time, was achieving peer appreciation without her father's money or her grandmother's "arrangements."

It was a new experience, one in which she thrived. She still had no boyfriends, other than classmates who considered her a friend but not a girl they wanted to date. She understood. It was 1953 and the popular girls were five-feet-two with pouter-pigeon breasts and a roundness to their bodies that enabled them to wear strapless gowns.

Marcella was a head taller than most of the boys at the university. Compounding her height was her sturdy build and the excess weight from years of compulsive eating.

It was during her junior year that she fell in love with her future husband.

Ed Schumacher was a senior and the university's star quarterback — a prime catch for any college girl. He was chased and caught by many. Ed was a fair student, preferring to excel on the football field and in the back seats of cars. His scoring record on and off the field was impressive. He was also clever and perceptive, knowing that the success he craved was not measured by the number of touchdowns he made or the amount of pussy he devoured.

Ed's family wasn't wealthy, they were middle class. Ed didn't plan on working in a factory as his father did. A football scholarship was his ticket to the university, and he knew the right connections would get him the power he craved.

Ed saw little use in attending his required courses, skipping as many classes as he could before being warned that even he, the star quarterback, was in danger of not graduating.

It was during a sociology lecture, as he sat in the back of the room and attempted to ignore the professor's droning voice that he spotted Marcella for the first time.

"Who in the hell is the fat broad?" he asked the student sitting to his left as Marcella and the professor engaged in what appeared to be a private discussion about Russian democracy or the lack thereof.

"You mean Marcy Grand?"

"Yeah."

"She's smart as hell, but with her looks it's a damned good thing her father's loaded," was the whispered response.

Ed looked at him quizzically.

"Carl Grand. You know, Grand Enterprises. Her father's the multi-millionaire shipyard owner."

"You're kidding."

"Nope. I suspect miss piggy is rolling in it, if you know what I mean."

Ed took another look at Marcella. She was nothing in the looks department, no two ways about it. But, if there was truth to what he'd just heard, he might have found his golden goose.

Ed's pursuit of Marcella was swift and intense. As soon as he'd checked out her father and found that upper society pivoted around the Grand name, he dumped his stable of easy lays and zeroed in on Marcella.

Marcella was overwhelmed with the attention from the tall, dark-haired handsome young man who so closely resembled her father's image in the yellowed photographs she kept in her nightstand.

Ed's attention forced her to take stock of her appearance and though she was disheartened by her obesity, diuretics hastened weight loss, a cosmetologist helped clear and conceal her facial blemishes, and a high-priced stylist cut and shaped her unruly hair. While she never would be a raving beauty, Marcella began to show the beginnings of stylishness.

Ed played the part of the perfect gentleman, bringing flowers for both Marcella and her grandmother. Mama Marcella was overjoyed at her granddaughter's attentive beau.

Even though he didn't press her, Marcella was more than willing to engage in heavy petting, or more, if that was what he wanted.

Ed ignored the snide catcalls of his friends and escorted Marcella to all of the university's social events. He turned down the chance to be king of the senior prom, choosing instead to escort Marcella and remain by her side all night. His pursuit of his golden goose was sharply focused.

Marcella and Ed made an impressive appearance at the senior prom, prompting some wits to remark that they looked like a matching pair of quarterbacks. It was after the prom, on a blanket spread along a lonely stretch of the causeway (the Corvette was far too cramped for sexual exploration), that Ed made love to Marcella for the first time. Marcella found the act to be no more fulfilling than when she'd been fourteen, but she moaned and sighed loudly, not knowing that Ed was also faking his appreciation of her Amazonian charms.

They were married two weeks after her graduation in a simple candlelight ceremony with only immediate family attending. That had been Marcella's fervent request. She didn't want the hoopla that weddings in her family's social circle demanded.

Ed's parents were reticent; afraid they might make a social blunder and embarrass their son. Marcella's father carried out his responsibility and walked down the aisle with her, although he didn't trust the sharp-eyed young man who had chosen his unattractive daughter for a wife. Marcella's grandmother cried great tears of joy and remembered back to her own daughter's wedding which caused her to weep even more.

After a Caribbean cruise, a gift from her father, they settled into their own suite of rooms in the Grand's Hyde Park mansion. Marcella's grandmother insisted they live with her, arguing that a twenty-five room estate for one old lady was ridiculous by anyone's standards. Ed agreed with Marcella's grandmother. He was more than ready to start enjoying the good life.

Marcella, enthralled with her handsome young husband, withdrew money from her trust fund and bought him the Thunderbird convertible he'd remarked about over dinner.

Ed soon found that Marcella needed only the slightest bit of prompting for expensive gifts to appear. And he felt not at all unscrupulous as he showed his pleasure for each new gift by mounting her and thrusting and plunging while she writhed and moaned beneath him. They both thought they knew what the other wanted.

They'd been married two months when Ed began what he called a serious search for proper employment. Much of his time, however, was spent in the apartment of a tiny blonde with big breasts whose specialty was giving head.

Marcella asked her father to hire Ed and her father agreed to talk with him. Ed was overjoyed to get an interview, assuming it would be only a matter of time before control of the entire Grand empire was passed to Marcella. Ed had every intention of knowing all facets of the business before that transfer took place.

Carl had strong reservations about his new son-in-law, despite his daughter's apparent happiness and his mother's reports of the couple's marital bliss, nor was he the type of man to leave anything to chance. He hired a private detective to do a thorough investigation of Ed and it wasn't long before the detective returned with a voluminous report.

There wasn't much about Ed that Carl didn't know before his interview, including the address of Francine's South Tampa apartment. Carl didn't find Ed's cheating to be objectionable, considering his daughter wasn't particularly attractive. And, after Anna's death, he decided that monogamy was very overrated.

As he approached his sixtieth year, Carl still had the distinguished good looks that drew young women and married socialites looking for extramarital excitement. A master of sexual technique, he knew what pleasures a woman responded to and he could usually unleash carnal passion in the most reserved of women.

Carl's own lust was satisfied by bedding children, preferring immature young bodies for his self-indulgent pleasures. When the need for children became too strong to ignore, he traveled to New York, Las Vegas, or Cuba where his contacts provided him unspoiled children at high prices.

Carl was determined to test the character of his son-in-law, offering him a job as a shipfitter. It was dirty, hot, backbreaking work but Ed recognized the challenge and took the job, putting in long hours until Carl moved him into accounting, and then out again into the shipyard, this time to supervise the construction and repair of the huge supertankers owned by South American conglomerates.

Carl was impressed with Ed's perseverance and hard work and rewarded him with an office and Rhonda, a young busty blonde. Carl knew from personal experience why Rhonda's nickname was "deep throat" and expected that Ed would soon take advantage of Rhonda's multiple talents.

With Ed working long hours at the shipyard, Marcella had more time on her hands than she wanted. She didn't complain since it had been her doing that got Ed into the family business and she, too, realized with her father getting older it wouldn't be much longer before he would turn over the majority of the business to to her.

Mama Marcella was eighty-seven when she died peacefully in her sleep. There was a large funeral and it was the only time Marcella ever saw her father cry. Marcella received a handsome inheritance from her grandmother, the mansion and its huge collection of fine art and antiques, as well as a healthy savings account accumulated through numerous years of her grandmother's penny pinching.

For the next year, Marcella oversaw the complete renovation and redecoration of the mansion. When the massive project was finished she searched for other ways to occupy her time.

It was a careless act by Ed that brought his cheating to Marcella's attention, a pair of flimsy black bikini panties hastily stuffed into a suit coat pocket and forgotten, then returned by the dry cleaners in a separate protective plastic bag. Marcella received the dry cleaning and put the suit away. Then she hired a private detective who brought her back a stack of glossy black and white photographs and a file thick with names, dates and places.

Marcella was faced with a choice to make. Confront Ed and take whatever came from the confrontation, or pretend ignorance and let things ride as they were. She weighed the possibilities and chose to keep her detective on retainer so she'd be apprised of Ed's activities.

As she had learned to do with her father, she now learned to do with Ed, cutting her emotional dependency on the one man she thought she could trust. From all outward appearances they were still the same loving, devoted couple seen at all important social events and galas. She was resplendent in sable and diamonds; he wore thousand-dollar suits and a diamond encrusted Rolex.

When Ed performed his obligatory mounting and thrusting, she still writhed and moaned as she had in the past, since it had always been pretend for her and now she realized it probably had always been feigned pleasure for him. And when she was alone in their immense bed she would move her hands over her body, and with a skill born of much practice, she would bring herself to orgasm, something Ed had never been able to do.

CANDY

Candy was young, blonde, generously endowed, and very beautiful. She had a ready smile, a mellow personality, and a kind word for everyone from the lowest paid worker to the CEO of any corporation for which she worked.

When she entered a room all eyes would turn to watch her settle comfortably into a chair, smooth her long blonde hair, position her rimless glasses on her pert nose, flip open her steno pad, and moisten the point of her pencil on the tip of her pink tongue. The ritual completed, she would look up, flash a glorious smile and the meeting could begin.

As a youngster, Candy hadn't been the most popular, or the prettiest, or the smartest. What she had been was cheerful. A cheerful little girl who grew into a cheerful teenager.

She was a late bloomer, as her family put it, not developing her luxurious curves until she was well into her teens. While her friends' biological time clocks were taking them into the responsibilities of adulthood at a rapid pace, Candy felt left out, believing there to be something wrong with her body's late development. Then she, too, matured. But, while her body developed its luscious curves, she was emotionally years behind her friends.

For Candy, it would have been a great service if sex education was a required subject in high school. It would have taken the teaching responsibility from Candy's mother, an inhibited woman who believed sexual relations were a marital obligation much in the same manner that cleaning floors and cooking were marital obligations. Candy's mother gave vague answers to Candy's vague questions. For Candy it was a puzzle. Exactly *how* were babies made?

When Candy's girlfriends got together for girl talk they never talked explicitly about sex. It was always that they had "done it" with the hunk from science class or they had "slept with" the gorgeous guy from the gas station. Candy was too inhibited to ask her friends exactly what "doing it" or "sleeping with" actually involved.

Candy's mother had a collection of sleazy confession magazines hidden in the back of her clothes closet, magazines written in the non-explicit yet titillating style of the 1950's, with the moral code of "good girls don't" that prevailed in confession magazines of that era.

Candy didn't realize her lush, ripe body was driving most of the young men in her classes to cold showers and masturbation in bathroom stalls. She was naive, too naive for her magnificent body.

When a classmate forced his tongue into her mouth one night she was scared that he'd made her pregnant. But time passed, and her belly didn't swell, and she began reading books her friends talked about, books like *Valley of the Dolls*, and *Peyton Place*, and eventually realized she'd been a fool. It had only been a kiss, her first French kiss at that, and she'd acted so dumb.

She came to the conclusion that sex was normal and natural, and quite expected between men and women. It was a period of awakening for her, the beginning of joy for the men who would pass through her life since she was eager to make up for lost time, accepting all dates, putting out in back seats, front seats, bucket seats, on beach blankets, anywhere, and almost any place. Candy was the darling of the football team, the basketball team, the baseball team.

Candy's mother continued to preach "Good girls are virgins on their wedding night. Virginity is the most precious gift a wife can give her husband." But Candy, seeing her mother's side of marriage, and her mother's attitudes, wasn't anxious to be married so the loss of her virginity wasn't important. She continued to spread her legs for any and every occasion.

"Sex is a sin!" preached Candy's grandmother who was a devoutly religious woman. And who, also, had buried eight husbands.

Unfortunately for serious suitors, and Candy had many, she did not feel any urgency to settle down with one man to make babies or to become the domestic creature so many of her friends had become.

The frustrated young men, while enjoying her luscious sexual charms, eventually met and wed other young women, though some of the young men continued to visit Candy after their marriages.

She knew there had to be more to sex than she was experiencing but, try as she would, it remained an act that excited her partners far more than it excited her.

Candy felt no need to go to college. She'd taken secretarial courses in high school and she aspired to no greater challenge than that of office work. With her blonde hair, sparkling blue eyes, voluptuous body, and her cheerful personality, she had no difficulty in getting secretarial jobs, particularly if the person doing the hiring was male. The jobs usually lasted until the boss' wife made a visit to the office.

While Candy was generous to her male admirers, she had no reservations about telling all to her girl-friends. She amused her female co-workers for hours with her stories, never malicious, always delightful, many times shocking, but mostly outrageous.

Candy took great pleasure in telling Marcella's group stories of the encounters she had in various business offices in the area. She wasn't inhibited in the least about sex and that seemed to remove the stigma from her promiscuity.

Unfortunately, as much as Candy tried, and as creative as she was, she was never able to achieve her ultimate goal, orgasm. But she knew, in her kindly heart of hearts, that if she tried enough men, enough times, and in enough ways, she'd find the right combination to unlock ecstasy.

Some women in the corporate world, such as Cissy, felt the only way to climb a corporate ladder was on their backs which is a risky position when climbing anything. Candy was not so ambitious. Servicing the chairman of the board or the president of a corporation suited her just fine. She had no illusions about becoming an executive, she left those lofty pursuits to women like Cissy.

She was happy when Marcella offered her a job as her social secretary. She was happier when Marcella said she would teach her the secret of the big "O."

"Your problem," said Marcella late one afternoon. "Is that you try too hard to give pleasure. You don't think about your own needs."

"But I do," said Candy.

"You've just finished telling me about the big jerk who balled you last night, who screwed his brains out, and kept asking if it was good for you too. When will they stop asking such a stupid question! You just told me you lied to him to make him feel good. You told me it was boring, you could have been having a doctor's exam for all you felt."

"That's true, but it wasn't his fault."

"No, you're right. It was your fault," scolded Marcella.

"Mine?"

"Look, any guy is still going to get his rocks off when you make it with him. It's up to you to tell him, instruct him, demand if necessary, that he do what pleases you. Then you let him come."

"I don't think—"

"Come on, you told me you've never once experienced orgasm. Is that right?"

"I haven't. At least I don't think I have."

"You'd know it, believe me, you'd know. If that's the case, you don't have the foggiest idea what really turns you on. That's where we start. Call it your homework assignment from your sex instructor."

"What do I do?"

"Didn't your mother teach you anything? No, I suppose not. Okay, first you go to the mall. There's an adult toy store with all kinds of nasty things for sale. You buy yourself at least two vibrators, and it's your choice as to the size you think appropriate, but I always believe bigger is better. Then go to the video store and rent at least three of the most x-rated movies they have. Then go home, lock the doors, close the drapes, turn on some soft music, dim the lights, take your clothes off, put a video on. Now, by this time you should have some inkling what to do with the vibrators, but let me emphasize it's perfectly acceptable to do whatever makes you feel good."

"I'm—"

"Don't interrupt. I know what I'm talking about. You just pretend you've got a couple linebackers in bed with you. Fantasize. Use the videos for inspiration, but let your imagination run wild. If you do, you'll unlock the secret needs you have, and you'll be able to act accordingly."

"How come you know so much about this?"

"My dear, I'm twice your age. Hopefully I've put some of those years to good use. Now go."

Marcella smiled bemusedly as Candy left. She was such a sweet girl, and so useful.

Candy was beaming radiantly when she came to work the next morning.

"Thank you," she whispered to Marcella. There was a glazed look on her face.

"Worked?"

"Incredibly!"

Sandra

"One can never be too thin," said Sandra as she cinched the leopard skin belt around her wasp waist and gave an extra tug to tighten the belt. She had worked hard to achieve her tiny waist, eighteen inches by her measuring tape, and, by god, everyone would damn well notice!

"Don't you think you're overdoing it just a bit, my dear?" Herbert whispered, as he wrapped a pudgy arm around her small waist and tried to pull her to him.

They were as different as night was from day, as pigs from pearls, and she loathed his touch. But until she could separate him from his vast fortune she forced herself to submit to him.

"Herbert! Don't! We're due at Marcella's in twenty minutes, and you don't want anyone to see me mussed, do you?" she wheedled as she deftly stepped from his awkward embrace. She knew he didn't give a damn what Marcella's friends thought, even though she knew he had immense respect for Marcella herself. But she also knew he would never refuse her wishes.

"You're right, my dear," he murmured as his arms dropped to his side.

There'd be time later, if the mood was right, when she'd join him in his bed and he'd hold her tenderly and be able to show her the magnitude of his love for her. The huge marquise solitaire diamond ring was nestled in its velvet-lined Cartier box, hidden in his nightstand. When she came to him he would merely have to reach to give it to her; if he went to her suite, it would be tucked into the pocket of his silk dressing gown. Either way, tonight they would make each other happy.

Sandra smoothed the folds of the silk dress. Black suited her perfectly, like a widow-in-waiting. She thought greedily about the surprise Herbert had in store for her later. Any night they shared a bed he made it worth her while — she saw to it.

"Herbert, darling," Sandra drawled seductively, "perhaps we should plan on an early evening?" She stroked the back of his thick neck with a perfect porcelain fingertip and smiled coyly.

Herbert brightened. It was the signal he had been waiting for — the signal she would share his bed. It was the game they played. It heightened the pleasure of sex for him. It gave her an excuse to be of service only when the mood struck her.

"You're so right, my dear, we should make it an early evening," he said and his heart raced as he anticipated the evening's pleasures to come. The diamond ring in its Cartier box had been in his nightstand for almost two months; finally he would have the joy of placing it on her finger. He licked his lips. She would earn that expensive ring; he'd make sure of it.

Sandra took another long look at her reflection in the mirror, patted her hair, picked up the leopard skin clutch from her dressing table and checked to see that she had the tickets for Marcella's little fundraiser. While Herbert stood silently waiting, she took a last look and approved of what she saw.

"Okay, darling, let's go see what Marcella is trying to save now," she purred.

Sandra didn't particularly care for Marcella. As a matter of fact, she had a rather intense dislike for the woman. But, Marcella was a major force in Tampa society and her approval was enough to make or break a newcomer. Sandra had been just such a newcomer and had the great fortune to benefit from Marcella's benevolent influence when she arrived in Tampa after her marriage to Herbert three years before. Marcella took her under her protective wing, showed her the ropes, taught her who the bitches were, who the chari- table members were. It had been an invaluable intro- duction for Sandra. Now she played by the rules and faithfully attended Marcella's functions, albeit reluc- tantly.

The Rolls pulled into the winding, tree-lined drive leading to Marcella's huge Hyde Park home. Marcella's family had lived in the grand old house since the turn of the century when her grandfather purchased the land cheaply, designed the spacious home for his young family, and found workers willing to construct his house at fair wages for a fair day's labor. The house had historical value because of its age, but it had little architectural design value since Marcella's grandfa- ther added and subtracted so much during the con- struction that the house had no fluidness or style.

They did not stay long at Marcella's. Herbert was preoccupied by thoughts of the evening which lay ahead, and Sandra was less than happy because most of Marcella's guests chose to ignore her newest Paris creation.

She took her time preparing for sex with Herbert. She felt no affection for him, no caring for the gentle old man who gave her everything she wished. Only his death would please her now.

Her maid drew bath water and scented it with one of her luxury bath oils. When Sandra finished soaking, the maid wrapped a thick terry towel around her as she stepped from the marble tub.

Sandra enjoyed being pampered but there was an extra excitement to having the young girl touch her body as she patted on fragrant powder.

She studied the girl's lush figure and tried to imagine how her thrusting breasts would taste. Would the girl pull away if she were to unbutton the top of the white uniform and cup the inviting breasts in her hands, run her fingers over the full nipples, and then suck as though she were a baby at her mother's breast?

She knew the girl was watching her as she turned for her back to be powdered. Oh how she wanted to rip the girl's uniform and expose that tender young body and search with her tongue for the spot she knew would turn the girl into a writhing, moaning woman. She knew how to make this young girl a woman, her woman. And she'd much prefer spending the night with her than with Herbert. Or even Greg. But, tonight had already been promised to Herbert. She sighed deeply.

"I'll wear the peach negligee tonight."

Sandra let the diaphanous material slide over her body with a hiss. As she looked at her reflection in the full length mirror and ran her hands along her body, she looked up and caught Janet staring at her. Their eyes locked.

"You are so beautiful," Janet whispered and then lowered her head.

Sandra reached over and patted Janet's cheek and cupped her chin, raising her head so their eyes again were level.

"I'm certain, my dear, you're just as beautiful," she responded. "One day soon we shall see, won't we?"

Janet's eyes widened and she nodded her head slowly. "Yes, ma'am," she said softly.

Sandra looked down at Janet's breasts straining against the material of her uniform and then looked into Janet's eyes. A blush spread across Janet's face.

"Get along now." Sandra turned back to the mirror. "I won't need you until the morning."

The young maid bowed and quietly left the room.

She had one last ritual to perform, the most important and one that had to be done in private, before going to Herbert. Locked in the center drawer of her massive antique dressing table was a solid gold vial she kept filled with Greg's premium grade cocaine. She carefully poured some of the fine white powder onto the mirrored dressing table top, cut and shaped it with a razor blade, and, using the solid gold straw, inhaled deeply, drawing one line into her right nostril and the second line into her other nostril.

It took only a few seconds for her to feel the cold rush as the coke raced through her system, deadening as it went, and then the burst as it reached her brain, and the feeling of elation and well-being she always got from high grade snow.

Now she was ready for Herbert. She could tolerate his obscenely fat body, his clumsy efforts to satisfy her. He would get his money's worth tonight, and she would get her payment, the exquisite marquise diamond ring in his nightstand.

She knew all the secrets in the house, or at least she thought she did.

DINNER PARTY

"It's a lovely party, don't you agree, dear?" Marcella asked Ed as she gazed around the room at her guests.

"Umm? Oh, yeah, sure," Ed responded as he attempted to avoid Cissy's stare. This was no place for her to make a scene but, knowing Cissy's state of mind, he figured she was ripe. About as ripe as her body.

"You're not listening to me," chided Marcella. "What — or who — has you so distracted?"

"Oh, uh, what were you saying?"

"I was saying too bad Herbert and Sandra had to leave so soon."

"They were here long enough for that little bitch to insult two of my most important clients — and then get angry when no one made a big hoorah over her fancy new dress."

"Ed, darling, you just don't understand Sandra. She's not like the rest of us, born to the manor, so to speak."

"I still don't get it," grumbled Ed. "Why the hell did Herbert marry a whore like that? With his money he could have gotten the best."

"My dear, perhaps she's a real dynamo between the sheets," whispered Marcella.

"Dynamo!? Why marry it when he can buy it?" exploded Ed.

"Shhhhhhh!"

"She's too damned skinny! No, she's malformed. That's not appealing."

"If you'll remember, she was quite the fresh pretty young thing when he brought her home," Marcella chided.

"Yeah, then she starts humping that tennis bum and dropping weight. He's probably the one who's supplying her with the nose candy, too."

"My, my, so it is true."

"What?" asked Ed sharply.

"Men do gossip as much as women," laughed Marcella.

"It isn't gossip. It's staying informed."

"Oh, I'm glad you made that distinction for me. I can pass it on to the girls when we get together. Let me make sure I have this right, though. As I understand it, women gossip and men stay informed? Is that it?"

"Don't you think you've had enough to drink?"

"Oh, quite the contrary, I believe I'm ready for another," said Marcella as she drained the champagne from her glass, placed the empty glass on a server's tray and take a full glass.

Ed pivoted to keep Cissy within his line of vision. Marcella watched him as he stared at Cissy.

"Pretty girl, isn't she?"

"Who?"

"Oh, come on, you know who. That lovely girl who works for you, Miss Turlington."

"I hadn't really paid much attention." He slowly sipped his drink.

"My dear, you may be getting older just like the rest of us, but your eyesight hasn't completely gone yet. That one looks like quite a good piece, and it appears your old buddy Damien is making a play to get a taste."

Having Ed's mistress at the party amused Marcella. Ed always had a mistress, and she stopped caring years ago. Now she took perverse pleasure in watching him struggle to control his rage as other men pawed his "trollop-de-jour" as Marcella called them. They were faceless creatures from the same mold: lush bodies, empty heads.

Cissy was the latest in Ed's long line of conquests, which was the only reason Marcella invited her to her party. It was another way to make Ed squirm.

Marcella knew Cissy was different than the others, there was more shark in her, more animal instinct for survival. And Marcella found that invigorating in an adversary. She always enjoyed a good, dirty, claws-bared cat fight.

"Ed, really, maybe you should go rescue the poor girl."

Marcella knew Ed was trying to avoid Cissy. It was obvious he was trying to get rid of her and she wasn't ready to be dumped. This was the part of Ed's cheating that amused Marcella the most. Let the bastard squirm, she thought.

"You're right," Ed sighed loudly. "Looks like Damien's had a little too much booze and his wife will kill him if she sees him with another woman."

"Yes, dear, time to play white knight."

Marcella drank slowly of the perfectly chilled Dom Perignon Rosé and watched as Ed took Cissy by the arm and guided her out onto the terrace. Neither of them were smiling. Serious time, thought Marcella.

"Okay, you son of a bitch!" spat Cissy as she spun away from Ed's hold.

"Keep your voice down!"

"I'll shout if I want to — daddykins!"

"Shut up," he hissed. The terrace was empty but he couldn't chance someone coming upon them.

"Oh, sure, I'll be glad to shut up, papa," Cissy declared. "Just as soon as you tell that magnanimous dowager you're married to about us. And don't forget to tell her about junior."

"You're trying to ruin me, aren't you?"

"Hey, papa, you're the one who told me we had the greatest love the world has ever known, and all that other trite crap. And I'm the one carrying our precious little bundle, remember?"

"You don't let up, do you?"

"Let up? You made me a lot of promises — and I intend to make sure you keep them all!"

"Oh, there you two are," said Marcella from the doorway. "Hope I haven't interrupted something important."

Ed looked panicked and Cissy started to speak but changed her mind.

"Well, I must see to my other guests," said Marcella as she turned and went back inside.

"We'll talk about this later," Ed said as he followed after Marcella.

"Yes, we will," called Cissy. "Yes, we will."

Cissy was sitting by herself when Candy came onto the terrace from the gardens. Candy had overheard the entire exchange between Ed and Cissy and would duly report it to Marcella later. Now it was time for her to pry what more she could from Cissy.

"Hi," Candy said cheerfully as she sat down across from Cissy. "Is this seat taken?"

"Oh, hi. No."

"You look down. Anything the matter?"

"No, not really," said Cissy.

"Well, if I can be of help—"

"I said there's nothing wrong!" snapped Cissy. She looked up and saw the hurt look on Candy's face.

"Hey, don't you get those kind of days?"

"Sure," replied Candy. "And it really sometimes helps to talk with someone."

"So, okay, I'm a little upset. Now, can we talk about the weather or something?"

"Man trouble?"

"Why do you ask that?"

"Oh, just because that seems to be the only problem that I can't solve," said Candy. She looked up and smiled. "They're really more trouble than they're worth, you know."

"Yes, don't I know."

"Then it is a man."

"Okay, yes. A married man. The lying bastard won't tell his wife he wants a divorce and now I'm prego."

"How terrible!" Candy put a hand on Cissy's arm.

"Yeah."

"What are you going to do?"

"Do? Well, I've considered slitting my wrists, shooting him, or going to his wife myself. I don't know which would be worse."

"If it was me—"

"Go on," prompted Cissy. "I'm curious. What would you do?"

"Well, I was going to say I'd tell his wife. But then if she didn't care—"

"Didn't care? How could any wife not care?"

"Listen, a few years ago, I fell in love, big time, with my boss. He was fantastic. Took me to nice places. Bought me jewelry, sexy lingerie, funny stuffed animals, sent me lots of flowers. I was sure I'd found the perfect man."

"Good in bed?"

"Well, as good as any of them have been," said Candy.

"And?"

"I knew he was married. He'd told me about his frigid wife and their loveless marriage."

"Same song, second verse."

"Kind of. We made plans. Actually, I made plans and he just agreed with whatever I said. I was too blind to realize he was just humoring me. And then, one weekend when he has to stay home because his wife, and here's the really great part, is dying of cancer, I go to a movie with a girlfriend and there he and his terminally ill wife are — two rows up from us. And the kids. Talk about a bummed-out feeling."

"So he was out with his wife. What's the problem?"

"She wasn't dying! She wasn't ugly, she wasn't any of the things he had told me about her. She was really quite pretty and a couple days later I pretended I was selling cosmetics and went to their house after he left for work."

"You're a gutsy little broad."

"Being in love makes you do stupid things. Anyway, she let me in and we talked. Just generalities at first. You know, she actually knew who I was. It almost blew my mind. I felt so stupid. Then she told me about the others. Then I felt even more stupid."

"Sounds like she was the stupid one to put up with that scum," said Cissy.

"She'd already thought it out. She told me that when she first found out about his girlfriends she'd demanded a divorce. He begged, pleaded, said he'd never love anyone but her, he'd never do it again—"

"Ah, same song, third verse."

"Exactly. So she believed him, took him back and things settled down until he got careless and she found out he was cheating again. But she didn't say anything. She'd already weighed going through a divorce and decided she would rather take the security his name provided than try to make it on her own. And there were the kids, she figured they needed a father."

"So what about you?" asked Cissy.

"I was out in the cold. She was a nice person," Candy said. "He wasn't worth it."

"You didn't make any trouble for him?"

"No, there didn't seem to be any point," responded Candy.

"And you kept working for him?"

"Oh, no, that was impossible. Whenever I looked at him, I saw a snake."

"I make them pay," stated Cissy.

"Pay?"

"You know, money, the great equalizer, that makes them hurt the most," Cissy's eyes gleamed.

"And you're going to make the guy that's got you upset, you're making him pay?"

"He will. And big. But hey, there's a party going on!" Cissy got up and started across the terrace. "Well, come on, I saw a couple live ones inside an hour or so ago."

"See, talking did help to cheer you up even though I did most of the talking!" Candy followed Cissy into the noisy room. She had a lot to tell Marcella.

Cissy

He had been rough the first time they had sex. She could look back and say it hadn't been very good, at least not for her. It didn't get better, but Ed thought he was wonderful and she didn't disagree with him. She never disagreed with him — at least not about sex. She let him think he was the best.

She let all her lovers think they were marvelous even though the best were the faceless bodies she seduced — supermarket bag boys, lifeguards, hitchhikers, construction workers, truck drivers. She used them as she had once been used. Quick and nasty. Her blue collar lovers gave her sexual pleasures none of her sophisticated lovers could.

Ed's reputation was legendary throughout the company. He'd fucked most of the secretaries who worked for him. Most thought sleeping with him would help their careers while all it did was get them more night work as Ed spread the word about who spread their legs.

Cissy interviewed for the office assistant job wearing a minimum of makeup, large glasses, a dark blue business suit, a white no-nonsense blouse, and her dark hair pulled into a severe bun at the nape of her neck.

The office manager, a fairly attractive woman in her late thirties had been unimpressed, therefore not intimidated by her looks, and she was hired based on her typing and shorthand skills. Her other skills she would use later.

The first week Cissy downplayed her looks so she could learn the power structure within the corporation. Ed paid little attention to her when she brought his coffee to him every morning.

She manipulated the game her way. Early to work, late to leave, a volunteer for any job. She memorized budget files, reviewed stockholder reports, and learned everything she needed to know about how the company and its executives functioned. She learned who was in power, who she needed to use, who she would need to get rid of when they became dangerous to her plans.

Monday of her second week she wore a clinging pale pink silk dress with several buttons open at the neckline to expose the promise of gorgeous breasts.

Her high-heeled strappy sandals made her firm buttocks move invitingly under the taut silk — the Marilyn Monroe trick of wearing one heel a half-inch higher gave her a pronounced wiggle as she walked. Her thick raven hair tumbled around her shoulders. Her makeup was expertly applied. Gone were the hideous eyeglasses, a camouflage to hide her luminous emerald-green eyes.

Ed looked up to grunt his normal "thanks" and spilled the hot coffee into his lap. She made a demure response, picked up a handful of tissues and began blotting the coffee in his lap — feeling the growing bulge as she mopped, knowing his eyes were staring down her bosom.

He sat as if in a daze until she finished, his tongue darting out of his mouth to wet his lips as he continued to stare at her breasts. "That's fine, thank you," he said in a thick voice as he jolted himself upright. "I shouldn't have been so clumsy." He moved to hide the bulge in his trousers from her frank stare.

She flashed him a smile, turned and slowly walked out of his office. She knew the effect she was having on him. It was the same effect she had on most men. She would watch them turn to stare at her and she could feel her back straightening, the swaying of her hips, the arching of her neck, and the little pout of her lower lip. It was instinctive, something she could control like an on-off switch. If she was in a particularly bitchy mood she'd switch on and tantalize construction workers, the grocery boy, and the telephone repairman. Some she'd bed if it suited her.

She stopped, turned slightly so Ed could see the tugging of her breasts and buttocks against the fragile silk. She lowered her head ever so slightly and smiled again.

"I'll bring you a fresh cup of coffee," she whispered huskily. With a well-practiced toss of her luxurious ebony mane she turned and was gone. She knew he was still staring at the spot where she'd been standing.

The rest of the day he made numerous trips past her desk, glancing over her shoulder, staring at her with a puzzled look as if he was trying to understand why he had never noticed her before. But, he wasn't the only one acting the fool that day or in the days that followed. The other men in the office were also finding a myriad of excuses to walk by her desk and ask her questions, anything to get her attention. But the game called for her to ignore them all until she was ready.

As the drab office assistant she had been accepted by the other women and she heard enough gossip to know who was doing what to whom, as well as when and where.

The first week she learned everything she needed to know in order to start her corporate climb. The second week she took the first step although it had been a bit trickier than she expected since she hadn't counted on Ed having a wife like Marcella. There was always a wife, and they all reacted the same way— until Marcella.

Cissy had no doubts Marcella knew Ed was unfaithful. It was even possible she knew Cissy was the woman. But Cissy was confused by Marcella, the rich bitch who lived in a big house, drove fancy cars, and wore designer clothing and a wealth of expensive jewelry. Why should the woman be so eager to include Cissy on the guest list for her parties? It didn't make sense.

"You worry too much, my pet," Cissy whispered to herself. "You wanted to be a part of the rich and famous, and now you worry that there's a catch. Go with the flow, pet. Go with the flow and pray the bastard doesn't make you ruin yourself having his kid."

She undid the thin silk sash, let it drop and shrugged her shoulders so the pale peach silk wrapper fell slowly to the bedroom floor. She ran her hands slowly over her smooth white thighs, up and across her taut stomach.

Her breasts were tender and swollen, the tell-tale sign of her pregnancy. It was still too early to worry about camouflage clothing — if the son-of-a-bitch forced her to have the kid. She was ready to play hardball with him, file a paternity suit, and do whatever it would take to shake the dollars out of him.

DADDY'S GIRL

"Daddy's going to take care of his baby girl real good."

The nightmare started when Sandra was nine years old. For six years, as her young body was brutally ravaged by her father, his friends and business acquaintances, she plotted her escape —and her revenge.

Her mother turned her head to the loathsome debauching of her only child. As long as her husband left her in peace, she didn't care nor did she want to know what he did to Sandra. Jesus was the only man she heeded or needed.

The onset of puberty increased the attention she received from her father and, as much as she tried, she couldn't hide the budding breasts or new round curves of her young body.

She had no school friends. Many of her classmates' fathers already used her on a regular basis. The sons would also have liked to partake of her body but most were afraid of their fathers. There were special occasions when some sons were permitted to use her — she was a favored "gift" for birthdays and graduations. The young men took her while their fathers watched and offered suggestions and encouragement.

When "outsiders" at school asked her for dates, her father made certain they never asked a second time.

Sandra knew what was happening to her was wrong. And yet, was it? He was her father. Her mother didn't object. She had no girlfriends to talk to, and even if she had, she felt certain it was not the type of subject young girls discussed.

Her junior high school counselor was an old prune-faced woman who screamed profanities at her when she tried, in the beginning, to ask if fathers were supposed to do certain things to their daughters.

She had to be wrong. And, yet, as she grew older, she read books and learned the meanings of "incest" and "rape." Then she knew. But who would believe her? Her father, as vile as he was with her, was one of the most respected men in their small Midwestern town. He was president of the bank, a deacon in the church, a city councilman. And the other men. The sheriff, the judge, other influential businessmen.

Her father blamed her for getting pregnant even though neither he nor any of the others used protection. The doctor who performed the abortion was one of the men who used her regularly — and he didn't charge for the professional service rendered. She cried afterward and her father beat her before climbing on top of her.

He didn't know she had a butcher knife hidden under her pillow. As he climaxed, she plunged the knife deep into his chest.

She hitched a ride with a young trucker. He figured she was a runaway but it didn't matter to him — as pretty as she was, and as horny as he was, why shouldn't he be accommodating?

She left him at a Las Vegas truck stop and got a ride into town with a local. She washed dishes and waitressed in coffee shops to pay for a room and to buy some clothes.

She soon found Las Vegas was full of displaced people like herself who were trying to escape going-nowhere lives. They all had a common thread, they wouldn't talk about where they'd come from or why they'd left. For them, they were born the day they arrived in Vegas.

She wasn't breathtakingly beautiful, but her youthful sensuality was more appealing than the hard-faced hookers who worked "Glitter Gulch" as the downtown area was known. And, so, she worked the men in the casinos, careful not to be too obvious.

When she had saved enough, she moved into a small apartment on the fringes of the "Strip" and worked the better casinos under the watchful eyes of the pit bosses. She learned not to spend too much time at any one casino. And she obeyed the cardinal rule: don't distract a high roller unless the house gives approval first. Her look was pure, virginal — though her sexual skills were diverse enough to please even the most demanding of johns.

In time she took in a roommate, a statuesque underage showgirl named Star. In a moment of mindless passion they fell in love. It shocked them both. Not so much that they could want each other so voraciously, but rather that they still had enough emotion within themselves to feel love for another person.

And so they survived.

When she left Las Vegas, she left without telling Star she was leaving. Saying goodbye would have been much too painful so she packed her scant belongings and left while Star was working. She knew Star could get along without her. And, with the new life she had planned for herself with Herbert, there was no room for Star.

As she settled back into the soft leather interior of the Rolls, Sandra remembered the first time she met

Herbert. She took an instant dislike to the obscenely fat old man smoking a foul-smelling cigar.

"Pure Havana, $30 each, I have them wrapped to my own special formula," the awful little man said as he waved the odious thing in her face. They were standing by one of the high limit roulette tables at Caesar's Palace.

She had been standing to the side of the table hoping to make a connection, take a high roller from the table for a half hour of fun and games, and then go on to Tropicana or Flamingo and find another high roller who needed a break from the gaming tables.

She'd worked Vegas long enough to know she was welcome to work the casinos if she didn't spend too much time in any one casino. There were rules to be followed; she followed them to the letter.

Her technique was always the same. She would find a player who was doing moderately well, who'd been at the tables for a while. She'd glance at the pit boss and when she got his attention she'd shift her eyes back toward her prospective john. Either the pit boss would give a slight nod or he would ignore her.

If she got the nod, she'd move to the side of the player, lean so she put the slightest pressure on his arm to gain his attention. The john saw a beautiful young girl, surely not old enough to be in a casino, looking in wonder at the wheel and the stacks of chips.

After he explained the game to her and perhaps gave her a few chips to play, they would go to his room and the sweet little country girl and the big city gambler (didn't they all think of themselves that way?) would tear up the sheets.

She'd leave the casino with cash and as many casino chips as she could safely pocket. She stayed by the high stakes tables where the chips were much larger denominations and she would pocket as many as four or five $1,000 chips while the john was busy looking down her dress or copping a feel.

Now she had to contend with this gross little man waving his horrid cigar under her nose in an attempt to get her attention. She sighed. If it weren't such a slow night she'd ignore him, move to another table or another casino, but she'd already tried the Flamingo and Bally's. Other than cheap conventioneers, the strip was dead. She smiled weakly and waved a thin pale hand at the air in front of her face.

"Please, I'm allergic," she said and gave a couple little hiccupping coughs.

"I'm sorry!" he seemed genuinely apologetic and dropped the cigar into a half empty cocktail glass abandoned along the rail. She heard the hiss and saw a small cloud of steam rise from the glass.

"Really, I always forget. Not everyone has the nose I have," he touched the side of his nose with a pudgy finger and raised his eyebrows as if asking a question. "Maybe it's good not so many people have the big noses, huh? It's alright now?"

She nodded. Without the cigar he was almost tolerable though she would have preferred someone more physically attractive. But, she reminded herself, not everyone could have a body like Star's. And this was work, not play.

"I'm sorry for making such a fuss," she apologized and smiled shyly at him. "I'm just visiting for a couple days before I go back home, and I was curious about how anyone can know what to bet. I've never seen such a confusing game." Of course she knew how to bet! Why else did her money go so quickly. She knew how to bet all right, she just didn't know how to win. Not smart for someone who worked in Vegas.

"You just watch me and you do what I do," he instructed as he handed her a half dozen chips. She recognized their denomination immediately. She was holding $6,000.

"You put your chip on the red or the black, don't worry what number," he said.

She placed a chip on red.

"All bets down, ladies and gentlemen," said the unsmiling man at the wheel. "All bets down. All betting is closed." He gave the wheel a well-practiced spin.

Sandra watched the wheel. She felt roulette was a fool's game since the wheel could be controlled by the house. But, for the high spending fat man she had to give a good performance. She turned and smiled timidly at him then turned back to watch the wheel. The ball bounced and she heard the clacking sound as it moved and finally stopped on black. He had 10 chips on black.

"Let it ride," he said.

She put another of her chips on red.

Black won again.

Again he let his stack of chips ride and again she bet one chip on red. It was black for a third time.

"Little lady, unless you take some chances in this world, it gets to be mighty boring," he whispered to her.

He let the small fortune in chips remain on black and she put her three remaining chips on black next to his. For a fourth time the ball clacked and jumped and finally landed on black.

She squealed and clapped her hands together in a display she figured he'd appreciate and he laughed at her feigned naiveté.

"And, now, little girl, we take our winnings and go some place nice and have some dinner. Okay?"

He motioned to the attendant to gather up his chips and cash them in for him. He flipped a couple chips to the man at the wheel. In less than 15 minutes he'd turned $10,000 into $80,000. And she still had the $6,000 he'd given her to play.

"Yes, I'd like that," she said with a little smile. So here comes pay back time, she thought.

But it hadn't been the evening she expected. He took her to the Japanese Steak House for which Caesar's was famous and they had a delicious leisurely meal with liberal amounts of Saki to keep the mood festive and light. He asked her a lot of questions about herself then told her much of his personal history at her insistance.

Sandra told him her standard story, the one she used whenever some john needed to turn her into more than just a quick trick.

She told him about her mom and dad back in Des Moines, about her younger sister who sang in the church choir and her older brother who was in the Navy on a submarine. She told him about her high school sweetheart who wanted to marry her when they graduated and how she refused, wanting to see some of the world first. So she was heading to San Bernardino to stay with her grandmother and hopefully get a job, maybe something to do with the movies. Which brought her through Las Vegas for a short visit.

She was quick to point out that she'd only been in town for a couple days and she was leaving to go to her grandmother's the day after tomorrow. A nice touch, she thought, going to live with her grandmother, it sounded so wholesome and pure. Her johns appreciated the image.

He said he was in Las Vegas with business associates who were high stakes baccarat players. He himself didn't care for gambling although he'd place a few bets at roulette, play a little blackjack and occasionally toss the dice.

He lived in Florida and owned a successful trucking business, his wife had died five years before, his kids were grown and lived away from home, and home was a large, three-story, twenty-room house that overlooked the water.

She listened as he talked and realized she had finally found the perfect john, her meal ticket off the Strip. This was the proverbial golden goose, tantalizingly close for her plucking.

After an excellently prepared and attentively served meal, they went to the lounge for drinks. They sat in a booth in a dark corner and he reached over and patted her hand.

"You're a nice young girl, not like the two-bit hookers in this town," he said scowling at two buxom blondes perched on nearby bar stools. "You go stay with your grandmother, take some college courses, marry a nice doctor, and have lots of babies."

She took his hand and cupped it in both of hers and traced the lines in his palm. She knew it would take a bit of work but if she played her cards right she just might become the next Mrs. Herbert Bianci, young society matron. Mrs. Sandra Bianci, she thought. Not a bad ring to it. And it sounded a damn sight better to her than Sandra Holdorf.

She knew she looked good, dressed in a soft, virginal-white cashmere skirt and sweater combination that showed off her body without being vulgar. The sweater had a high neckline in front and a low draping back that left much of her pale skin exposed. Her dark ash blonde hair hung past her shoulders and was pinned back to expose her perfect ears on which were clipped tiny pearl earrings. She was an expert in applying the necessary creams, make-up bases, highlighters, blushers, shadows, mascara and light lip gloss that created her fresh schoolgirl look. She used no hairspray and only a few drops of Shalimar on her neck, behind her ears and between her breasts.

"My dear," said Herbert as she continued to trace the lines on his palm. "It's getting late and I have been taking up too much of your time. A pretty young girl should not be monopolized by an old goat like me." He started to draw his hand away and she grasped it tightly.

"But I'm having such a good time," she said wistfully. "Actually, I've been very lonely since I got here and I've enjoyed talking to you. It's not like—" she lowered her head and traced circles with one finger on his palm. "Well, you're not like—"

"Not like what," Herbert asked, and when she wouldn't reply but continued to trace circles he pulled his hand away so fast it scared her. "You mean you've had some scum try to—" she placed a dainty hand over his mouth.

"Please," she whispered, the tears filling her eyes on cue. "Nothing happened."

"Dirty, slimy, scum! Don't know how to treat a lady!" He pounded the table with his fists and nearby lounge patrons turned to stare.

"Please, please, Herbert," she pleaded. "I'm okay, nothing happened. Please, can we leave?" She started to rise from the booth.

The barmaid was hurrying to their booth and he flipped a fifty onto her tray without waiting for change. He had a suite at Caesar's and she fully expected they would finish the night together. Instead, he put her in a taxi, handed the driver a twenty and told him to take her to the Sahara, where Sandra had told him she was staying. He promised to call her in the morning and take her for a tour of Hoover Dam and Lake Mead.

Once the taxi pulled away from Caesar's entrance, she directed the driver to her small apartment complex on the fringe of the Strip and while the cabbie waited for her she packed some clothes into a bag, threw essentials into a cosmetics case and then had him take her to the Sahara.

Two days later, in the "We Have Just Begun" wedding chapel she became Mrs. Herbert Bianci. And that night she lost her virginity for the last time.

Sandra had been determined to erase all traces of Sandra Holdorf. She was slim during her Vegas days, but with her new identity as a young society matron, she dieted unmercifully until she was a perfect designer size 2, even though Herbert complained that she was too thin. In reality, she was gaunt, but, as she consoled herself to stop the hunger pangs, within high society one could not be too rich or too thin.

Her hair was cropped and shaped to curl under at chin length, her natural dark ash color lightened to pale platinum; her lush bangs brushed back exposing a high forehead accented by a pronounced widow's peak.

Her weight loss removed all traces of baby fat from her face and her high cheekbones, classic nose, wide-set hazel eyes, and cupid's-bow mouth created the illusion of a well-bred, monied woman. Couturier clothes, elegant jewelry, and a reserved but haughty demeanor tied the illusionary package together. The traces of Sandra Holdorf, Las Vegas whore, were obliterated.

Herbert reached for Sandra's hand and she shook herself from her trip back in time. She wasn't sorry she married Herbert. He was old, his health wasn't great, and the way he kept eating there was no doubt his heart would give out quickly enough. Then she'd be free and rich. In the meantime, she had tanned, muscular Greg for Wednesday "tennis lessons."

Greg, tall, tanned, and sexually talented, not only knew how to satisfy her, he also kept her supplied with high grade snow, without which she could never endure Herbert's touch, nor could she so easily continue to control her weight.

Sandra held no illusions about exclusivity with Greg. She had known many others of his type when she worked the Strip. He was after the money and the contacts his tennis pro job provided. Being exceptionally good looking and sexually talented were necessary qualifications. To Sandra, Greg was a disposable commodity, and it was well known Greg was looking for his own "golden goose."

Sandra's daily schedule left little time for Herbert, as had been her original intention. When she met him in Las Vegas she took an instant dislike to him, a dislike that grew in proportion to the wealth and status he bestowed upon her during the three years of their marriage.

She hated him for the power he had over her but she considered her value to him and, as she believed any intelligent businesswoman would, she made certain she was sufficiently compensated.

It was a good business arrangement, reasoned Sandra. As a Las Vegas prostitute she might have had a few more good years before the hard lines would have formed and the casino managers would have not so politely told her to work downtown — Glitter Gulch — where the aging and cheap whores stood on street corners and disease was an every trick hazard. Or she could have moved into one of the legal brothels that the state licensed and monitored. Until Herbert her future had not been very bright.

No, better to take one steady job as Herbert's wife, enjoy the security, status, and control, and in time hope his heart gave out so she could bury him and get her hands on his money.

It wasn't a bad life, actually, since she had Greg who supplied her with primo snow and fairly decent sex, and now she would have Janet to fill the void left when she abandoned Star, Las Vegas roommate and lover.

Separate bedrooms were a priority when Herbert and Sandra married. With Herbert's day beginning at 5:30 a.m. with the first of many overseas phone calls, it had been easy for Sandra to plead her need for her own suite of rooms.

Herbert agreed to remodel a portion of the second floor, with Sandra choosing the decorator and decor, and in a matter of weeks Sandra was able to estrange herself from Herbert — except when it suited her to spend some time with him, and then she extracted equitable compensation for her time. Expensive jewelry she considered "equitable compensation," as well as no-limit charge accounts at major stores in and out of the state: Saks, Bergdorf-Goodman, Cartier, Gucci, De Beers.

Sandra's luxurious suite of rooms included a massive walk-in closet, a separate climate-controlled fur storage vault, a dressing area complete with beauty salon equipment, and thousands of dollars worth of make-up by Estee Lauder, Revlon, Lancome, Clinique, L'Oreal, Ultima and others. The ornate glass-front hutch was filled with expensive perfumes: Chanel No. 5, Joy, Shalini, Notorious, 24 Faubourg.

Her bath bordered on ludicrous: a huge room containing a French marble garden tub, gold-flecked dual wash basins with 24-carat gold fixtures, a professional tanning booth, an oversized shower outfitted in marble and gold, a bidet, a steam room, and a custom-made hot tub large enough for a party of twelve — should such an occasion ever arise.

While Herbert made sputtering noises about the cost of the bath, Sandra assured him all items were necessary to her health and happiness. Choosing not to refuse her, he paid the exorbitant bills and he contracted for additional modifications of which Sandra was unaware.

Sandra's canopied bed was a copy of a bed she had seen in an issue of *Elle*. The custom canopy and matching dust ruffle were sewn from $125-a-yard antique French lace. The same lace trimmed the pillow shams and satin comforter. Her sheets were imported from France and her head rested on only the softest and most expensive goose down pillows.

It was quite a change from sharing a dingy one bedroom apartment, shoplifting cheap cosmetics at the drugstore, and buying clothes at thrift stores. Life definitely was delicious and it was about to get even more so.

Secrets

Janet stood rigidly still as Sandra unbuttoned her uniform and slowly peeled it from her young body. Her eyes were wide with fear as she stood upright in the middle of Sandra's extravagant bedroom wearing only her cotton camisole, bra and panties.

Sandra pushed the camisole straps from Janet's shoulders and, reaching down, pulled the white undergarment over Janet's head. She stepped back once more and drank in Janet's lush beauty, her voluptuous breasts straining the cheap cotton of her bra. She moved close and wrapped her arms around Janet's immobile body while Janet took shallow gulps of air.

Sandra released the bra hooks and pulled the undergarment out of her way. She cupped Janet's breasts in her hands, looked into Janet's frightened eyes, smiled and then bent down to take the dark tip of a tender breast into her mouth. She sucked on the nipple until it became hard then moved to the other breast and sucked until she heard Janet make a low moan.

Sandra returned to the right nipple and circled it expertly with the tip of her tongue, then moved to the left nipple while her hands moved up and down Janet's body.

Janet was moaning softly and Sandra reached up and kissed her on her full lips then forced her mouth open and searched with her talented tongue. Janet wrapped her arms around Sandra's slim body.

Sandra pushed Janet's arms away and reached again for the full breasts with their fantastic dark nipples. She knew this would be the first of many wonderful meetings with the young maid, and she planned on training the girl well. They would both benefit, she'd see to it.

Sandra led the girl to the huge bed and told her to lie down. There was a look of fear mixed with lustful anticipation on the sweet young face.

Later, they lay quietly together, their appetites sated. It had been even better than Sandra thought it would be.

"Our secret?" asked Sandra and Janet nodded.

"Tomorrow?"

Janet nodded again and slid off the bed, picked up her clothes and dressed.

"Will that be all, ma'am?"

Sandra stretched languorously. "Draw my bath in an hour. Right now, I wish to nap."

"Yes, ma'am," replied the young maid as she started to leave the room, a quizzical satisfied look on her face.

"By the way," said Sandra. "You were delicious."

Janet blushed.

Sandra lay back, temporary quenched. Life was getting exceptionally delicious.

Hours later, having rested then dressed with meticulous care, she called for the Rolls. She felt good — time to buy something expensive for herself and maybe a little bauble for Janet.

"Hello, little darlin'."

Sandra's hand froze on the ornate doorknob. She knew the voice and she didn't want to turn and match it with the face from her nightmares.

"Come on, now, honey babe, turn around an' give your old daddy a great big hug." It was a malicious command.

She felt the adrenaline shoot through her body. Her hand gripped the doorknob tightly as her knees started to buckle. Oh, God, she thought, this can't be happening, please don't let it be happening!

"What's the matter, honey babe? Gotten too uppity to give your poor old father a big hug and a kiss?"

It was impossible! Absolutely impossible! He was dead! She knew. She killed him.

"Honey babe, turn and let me look at you," he commanded again.

She turned and as she looked into his mocking eyes the blackness closed in around her.

Sandra's life alternated from manic to depressive with her father's re-entry. Herbert had been delighted to allow his young wife's newly widowed father to move into the huge mansion, although he was unable to understand Sandra's despair at having her father in the house. Herbert decided the shock of her mother's death was too much for her fragile temperament to accept. It had been sad news that brought Charlie Holdorf to see his only child.

What Herbert could not explain was why Sandra had not tried to maintain contact with her parents after their marriage. And why had she concocted the story of her siblings?

For Sandra, each new day was terrifying. Her father was accepted into her new world with no questions asked. Here he was, the poor bereaved widower looking for moral support from his only beloved daughter — what a laugh! It had taken him less than one day to invade her bedroom and put her life into terrifying turmoil.

Charlie Holdorf was courted by the older society women, his presence at a party sure to turn it into an event to remember.

"Different like night is to day," was the comment repeated more than once when the ladies gathered to gossip. "How such a nice man could have produced such a horrid daughter," they clucked. "Children. You just never could tell."

With her father in the house, and Herbert being so solicitous, Sandra spent most of her time in her suite of rooms, pleading a variety of ills from migraines to intestinal flu. The times she was able to get away from the house she spent with Marcella or Greg.

"So my little darlin's got a pretty playmate."

Sandra bolted upright in bed and Janet stopped her ministrations between her legs, staring quizzically at the older man as he walked toward the bed.

"You just get back to what you were doin' at that honey hole, sweet thang," drawled Charlie as he laid a pudgy hand on Janet's bare rump and massaged the soft skin.

Janet looked at Sandra, saw her nod, and, her ass pointing skyward, Charlie's fingers poking and touching, she returned to Sandra's moist core.

"And I thought my little girl didn't know how to show her ol' daddy a good time," smirked Charlie as he bent over and took one of Sandra's rigid nipples in his mouth and bit down until tears coursed down Sandra's cheeks. He unzipped his trousers and pulled on Sandra's hair, forcing her to open her mouth.

And so the game changed. Charlie took to his room as much as Sandra took to hers. But Charlie didn't stay in his room; rather, he stayed in Sandra's room and choreographed sexual encounters for the three players.

Sometimes he was an observer, but mostly he participated when and how he knew it would hurt Sandra the most. Charlie found Janet an unexpected bonus, and so eager to please.

For Sandra, Charlie's reappearance had plunged her back in time to the frightening world of an abused nine-year-old. She needed her drugs to get through each day, and it became necessary to pay Greg huge sums of money for the additional snow and high volume of pills she demanded from him. That she no longer slept with him was of no concern to Greg — money was his turn-on, and he had enough aging society matrons to service as it was.

Sandra's mood swings resembled a berserk ping pong ball. One minute she would be gaily parading about in a new designer dress, and the next she'd be ripping the dress from her body and tearing it apart with her hands.

Marcella could see the change and wondered if it had something to do with Charlie's surprise appearance. Marcella took an instant dislike to Charlie, but she didn't vocalize her feelings to the group.

Candy told Marcella of Charlie's attempt to feel her up but Marcella wasn't surprised since most men, young or old, put moves on Candy at least once. But there was something wrong and she couldn't quite figure it out.

Lessons In Self Defense

"I'd call anyone stupid who married someone who locked her in a closet."

"Who did that?"

"I did. We were living together and he threw me in the clothes closet and put a chair up against it so I couldn't get out."

"You?"

"Yeah, do you believe it? I pounded and yelled and finally I got the clothes rod down. What a mess that was! But I kept banging it against the door and finally broke through."

"Sounds like he had some repair work to do."

"He rented the apartment so it didn't matter to him. He moved."

"And you still married him."

"I loved him."

"And now you're afraid of him."

"He's been making threatening calls to my office. I had my home number changed but he drives by."

"Listen, this is what you do—"

"I'm going to buy a gun. Someone told me to buy a .38, carry it unloaded, and point it toward him but not directly at him if he ever shows up."

"Listen to me, you can't carry an unloaded gun. I've got a .357, I can teach you how to shoot. We'll go to the police range."

"No, first you go to the Belleair Police Department and tell them you're new in town, that you have been having trouble with your ex-husband. That he's been threatening you, that he has a history of violent behavior. That way if anything happens—"

"A gun, you have to get a snub-nose .38 and keep it loaded with hollow point bullets."

"That's what I did, and they assigned a detective to me, he was so concerned he even gave me his home number so that if anything happened I could reach him even when he wasn't on duty."

"Hollow points, they do the job. And you don't hold the gun out like this."

"I was watching some police—"

"You grip it with both hands, hold it close to your stomach, spread your feet apart. If you hold the gun out then someone can grab it, but no one's going to be able to get this close to you before you can shoot."

"How come you know so much about guns?"

"I went to the police range when I got my divorce. They taught me. They put me in front of those big targets and showed me how to shoot. I can shoot with my gun down here, I don't even have to use the sights, and I can hit the target."

"But where do I buy a gun?"

"Wal-Mart."

"Wal-Mart sells guns?"

"There are other places. A pawn shop."

"No, you want a new gun. Just in case."

"I don't know anything about this. What would a snub-nose .38 cost me?"

"Well, I paid $235 for my .357."

"That gun can stop anything."

"I wanted something I felt secure with."

"Will you help me?"

"I told you I would."

"Where's the check?"

"I'll take care of it."

"Wait, we didn't come here for lunch so you could treat us!"

"Don't worry about it."

"I'll get the next one."

"I left a tip on the table."

"Well, I'm taking it back. She wasn't worth a tip."

Karen and Bobbi watched the three women leave the restaurant and then broke into fits of laughter.

"Do you honestly believe all that?" roared Bobbi.

"Lots of misguided females in the world," responded Karen. "I just don't want to be in their way."

"Sounded like a good argument for gun control, I'm sorry to say."

"I have to agree with you. But let's get to your problem — you did say it was a problem?" Karen asked.

"Yes, I think we've stepped into something deep and dirty. And you're a clear thinker, I trust you. But there's always another time. I enjoyed listening to those dimwits next to us. It serves as a reality check about the craziness around us."

"You're right. I forget sometimes that not everyone lives the way I do, thinks the way I do."

"The real world intrudes!" exclaimed Bobbi.

"Tell you what, let's go strolling. It's a gorgeous day for walking. We'll take a peek at the new spring fashions—"

"Ugh!"

"Okay. I forgot, you're not a fashionista," Karen chuckled. "Then let's go people watching and you can fill me in." Karen signaled for the check.

"Sounds good," Bobbi grabbed the check and handed the young waitress her gold card.

"I didn't expect you to pay. Oh, lord, sounds like a repeat from the dimwit table."

"No problem. You leave a fat tip and we'll call it even."

Karen placed a $20 bill on the table. Bobbi smiled.

Karen appreciated outings with Bobbi and she welcomed the chance to concentrate on problems other than her own.

LUNCHEON DATE

"I was terribly hurt that none of you came to my dinner party last night," Sandra pouted.

"My dear," scolded Marcella. "You must understand, we all live very full and busy lives. Don't we, ladies?"

"Sure, you're all so very occupied you can't take a little time out, a few lousy hours to spend some time with Herbert and me."

"Hey, I would have come," said Cissy.

"I didn't invite you," Sandra replied icily.

"Oh, goodness, my mistake!"

Once again they were seated at "their" table in the Garden Room. Waiters hovered a discreet distance away waiting for Marcella's signal to serve the appetizers.

"I sent you my regrets," said Karen softly.

"Oh, sure," Sandra whined. "You couldn't take time out from crying to come to my party but you've conveniently dried your tears long enough to come to Marcella's luncheon."

"Sandra!" Marcella roared. The waiters rushed to the table and she waved them away.

"It's okay, Marcella," Karen said in a soft voice.

"No, it's not!" responded Marcella. She knew Karen was still grieving for her husband.

"Yeah, Sandra, that was a terrible thing to say to Karen," scolded Candy. "Apologize. Tell her you didn't mean it."

"Now!" commanded Bobbi.

"Okay, okay. I'm sorry," Sandra replied contritely. "But you-all hurt my feelings."

"Always have to get the last word in, don't you?" Cissy asked. "And drop the phony drawl."

"Ladies, let's eat lunch before we all lose our appetites." Marcella gave the waiters a signal to bring the entree. Sandra was beginning to annoy her.

"Karen, if you had it to do all over again, would you have ever gotten married?" asked Candy.

"I don't know," answered Karen.

"Does that mean you wouldn't have gotten married at all?" asked Candy.

"I suppose it means that I don't know," said Karen softly.

"That's what I like, a straight answer," Cissy snickered.

Karen turned to face Cissy. "You've never been married. Why don't you tell us why."

"Hey, you're the one Candy was talking to."

"And you're the one who opened your mouth," said Marcella. "So why don't you tell the rest of us why you haven't tripped down the matrimonial path."

"I haven't wanted to," replied Cissy. "The right man just hasn't come along."

"You mean you haven't been able to pry the right husband away from his wife," said Marcella.

"The loss of personal identity," Karen said, cutting into the middle of a potential fight between Marcella and Cissy. They all knew Cissy was Ed's mistress.

"Personal identity?" asked Candy.

"Growing up as a person then getting married and becoming a part of another person. A second part, a lesser part," said Karen.

"You mean like being Mrs. John Jones instead of Karen Jones?" asked Candy.

"Yes, that, and more. It's an assumption that when a woman marries she is second to her husband's needs. Society's placement of a wife as an attachment to a successful man, an accessory like a house in the right neighborhood and membership in the correct country club."

"I've never felt that way," said Sandra.

"My dear," crooned Marcella. "You are a classic example of a successful man's accessory."

"I make Herbert happy," Sandra snapped.

"And so you should," said Marcella as she turned to wink at Candy.

"I'm glad to have people know me as Herbert Bianci's wife," Sandra continued.

"Particularly the jewelry stores," laughed Cissy.

"You should be so lucky," Marcella sniped at Cissy. She didn't particularly like Sandra, but she definitely loathed Cissy.

"I suppose that's why I won't marry Chris," said Bobbi. She wanted to stop the fight brewing between Marcella and Cissy. "I've seen too many of my friends get married under the best of conditions and then get submerged in the relationship. They get sidetracked and waylaid by being a wife and mother. Society just refuses to let married women excel as individuals."

"But women make up a great part of that same society," Karen said softly.

"Right, and women are busy sabotaging themselves," said Bobbi.

"We are? How?" Candy asked.

"Simple little ways," replied Karen. "Like my mother. She disliked Tommy as soon as he stood up to her. One of the reasons I married him, even knowing that he wasn't the best choice, is because my mother despised him so much. As much as she hated him, she kept pressuring me to have children, but for all the wrong reasons."

"Like what?" asked Candy.

"She said I was denying her the joy of grandchildren. When I tried to explain that I just didn't consider myself to be good mother material, she got angry, said I was selfish, and that I had to have children so I'd know how much she'd suffered as a mother."

"Wow! Bad reason!" exclaimed Bobbi. "She really told you that? She couldn't have been serious."

"I'm afraid she was deadly serious," said Karen. "Looking back, I think that my mother felt trapped by her necessary roles of wife and mother. During the forties and fifties it was, I'll admit, not the best time to be a woman who wanted more out of life than being Suzie Homemaker. She took her frustrations out on all of us, particularly my father and me. My father was the one who 'trapped' her in the wife and mother role and I refused to let her live out her fantasies through me."

"You're saying you weren't the perfect daughter?" asked Bobbi.

"I don't think there are any perfect daughters," said Karen. "Although it's taken me a long time to realize it, and to see that my mother's fantasies and dreams colored a great deal of how I looked at the role of mother. That's the biggest reason why I never wanted to be one."

"My mother was unhappy a lot," said Candy. "She used to tell me that she wished she'd been born a man. It never made sense to me. She kept talking about all the things she would have done if she were a man."

"My grandmother was happy in her role as surrogate mother to me," said Marcella. "But then, she was from another era altogether, before women started looking for identity outside of the home. I suppose I was lucky."

"I was, too," said Bobbi. "My aunt was quite a bit older when she 'inherited' me. She seemed very comfortable being a mother."

"Many women are, but they can make life miserable for the women who choose a childless lifestyle," said Karen. "When I was in my early twenties, before Tommy and I got married, I had a girlfriend I ran around with. Suzy was the kind of girl who fell in love with every guy she dated. I didn't stand in judgment because I couldn't prove her lifestyle was more damaging than mine, but, when she slit her wrists over a guy, I figured she wasn't as happy-go-lucky as she pretended to be. After her suicide attempt she quit her job and left town. Her family was glad to see her go, her kid brother was tired of defending her honor, and her parents were just tired of her. She wrote me a few times. She bummed around and spent a lot of time in a drunken haze." Karen stopped.

"So what happened to her?" asked Candy.

"She met a guy. Seems they had been leading parallel lives. They agreed to bury their individual pasts. They got married and she had a couple kids. Our last conversation she berated me for working, said a woman's place was to bear children, make a comfortable home for her husband. It was a real turnaround. She refused to work because she didn't want to have anyone else raising her kids and she planned on having as many kids as she could. I asked her if they could afford the expense of a large family since they were struggling to pay their bills and she said it didn't matter, what mattered was being a mother. When I talked about quality of life she criticized me, said I was money hungry, putting a career before a family. It wasn't a pleasant conversation and it was the last contact we had."

"Total rejection of what she was, sounds like to me," said Bobbi.

"Probably," Karen agreed. "She thought I was finding fault with her choices and she lashed out at me in self-defense. All I was asking from her was the chance to live my own life in my own way the same as she was doing. My mother hated Suzy up to that point.

Suddenly, Suzy was the type of daughter I could never be."

"But how does that answer Candy's original question about marriage?" asked Sandra.

"You've said you're happy with the role as Mrs. Herbert Bianci," said Karen. "You're also quite young. You may always enjoy the role you're in. And perhaps Herbert gives you enough freedom—"

"That's it!" cried Marcella. Karen looked startled. "You said the magic words!"

"What?"

"You said perhaps Herbert 'gives her enough freedom.' Why must a man give a woman freedom? Aren't we entitled to it? That's the whole damned problem facing women today! We sit back, assume it's the way it's supposed to be. The man always in the position of giving, letting, allowing. I'll tell you one thing, Ed learned a long time ago I wasn't going to accept a subservient role in our marriage."

"I can't imagine him trying," said Karen.

"Oh, on the contrary," said Marcella. "Marriage gave him instant access to my money and it didn't take him long to forget where the money came from. I found myself asking him for permission to buy this, buy that, go here, do this, do that. He assumed the role and I followed. Then, we were at a party and everyone was gathered around him, congratulating him on some big business coup and I'm standing in a circle of wives. One of them turns to me and whispers how lucky I am to be married to such a successful man. I told her it was actually the reverse, he was lucky to have married me since it was my father's money that made him so successful. I said it loud enough so Ed could hear me. We had quite a fight that night. He said I embarrassed him in front of his business and social peers. I asked what about me, how I felt?" Marcella stopped.

"What did he say?" asked Karen.

"He said with my looks it was a good thing I was rich."

Cissy snickered.

The table fell silent.

"I play a little game with Ed," said Marcella. "He used to not care if I spent time away from him, but now, whenever he's at home, he demands that I sit in the same room with him. He watches boxing on television, one of those 24-hour cable sports channels. He knows I hate sports. He gets home, turns on the TV, hunts me down and insists that I sit and watch the fights with him."

"What a horrid, horrid chore!" Cissy chided.

Marcella ignored her. "I've agreed to sit with him, but only if I can read. Then it turns into game time. He ignores me until I look down at my book or magazine, then he asks me how my day went, or what I think about this or that. As soon as I look up and start to give my opinion, he turns away and stares at the television. I look down at my book, he asks me another question. I start to answer and he turns away. It took me a while to catch on to what he was doing. To see if I was right, I'd look up and keep staring at the side of his face for five or ten minutes. Nothing. Not a word. I'd drop my head like I was reading, but I'd actually be watching him. He'd immediately start talking to me, trying to get my attention. I'd look up, he'd look away. I'd look down, he'd start talking."

"Why's he doing it?" asked Candy. In all their heart to heart talks, Marcella had never mentioned Ed's strange behavior.

"Maybe so I'll be glad when he leaves the house in the evening," Marcella turned to stare at Cissy.

"And are you?" asked Cissy.

"Am I what?" challenged Marcella.

"Glad?"

"Yes."

Cissy smiled. She planned to relate the entire episode to Ed. She doubted he would be amused.

"Jimmy won't be that way," said Candy.

"They're all that way, honey," said Marcella.

"Not Jimmy," repeated Candy defensively. Jimmy was the young mechanic who maintained Marcella's

Mercedes. He'd had a crush on Candy from the moment she brought the red SL in for routine servicing. He was in awe of her lush body, her beautiful face, her soft melodious voice. It was Candy who spoke to him first, asking simple questions about the car, allowing him the chance to ask if she'd like to go get a drink. He couldn't believe his luck when she said yes.

Theirs was an intense relationship with Candy as enthralled with Jimmy as he was with her. He was the complete opposite of the businessmen who'd used and discarded her for so much of her life.

"Maybe not Jimmy," agreed Bobbi. "And maybe you're ready for a man to take charge for a while anyway."

"Maybe," Candy said and she smiled wistfully. "Maybe I am." She'd begun to believe she'd never find a man to love, her life destined to be single sex and microwave meals for one. She'd been oblivious to him the first few times she'd driven the car to the repair garage. Then one day, as she was starting to leave, she caught him staring at her and he turned away in embarrassment. She was amused and surprised. Most men stared boldly at her and she instinctively could read their thoughts. This was different.

Jimmy had proven to be a wonderful change from the selfish sophisticated men of her past. He wrote her love poems and brought her wildflowers. And when they made love, it was at her insistence, and he gladly did everything she asked, and more.

Karen

Karen thought back to her last days with Tommy, the clean-up days.

"If you leave," he pursed his lips then drew out the rest of his words so they'd have maximum impact. "You won't ever be able to come back."

For two months Karen had been gathering her courage to tell him it was over, that she never wanted to see him again. Or maybe it had been the last ten years she'd been trying to tell him. It seemed as though she'd wanted to leave him for her entire life. How free she felt as they began their last dialogue as a married couple.

"You're making a big mistake," he said and squinted at her. "I'm your only anchor. Without me, you'll be lost."

It was difficult for her to keep from laughing. He was right about being an anchor, of course, holding her down at every step. Lost? She was the one who stayed with him during his fight with alcohol, she believed him when he swore he'd never drink again, and she was the one who cleaned up his vomit at 3 a.m. after he'd come home from the local bar in a drunken stupor, stumble down the hallway, empty his guts onto the floor mid-way to bed, then collapse in bed while her stomach threatened to empty as she cleaned up after him.

Lost? She was the one who had never smoked but who put up with his mental battering when he finally quit cold turkey from a five-pack a day habit after the spots showed up in his chest x-rays.

Lost? Hers was the steady paycheck while he hopped from job to job trying to decide what he wanted to make of his life.

Lost? If she didn't leave him she really would be lost. It was time to save herself from the walking death that would come from staying with him any longer.

"Who is he!?!"

She laughed. "There isn't anyone else! That's the toughest part you're going to have to comprehend. I've been completely faithful to you all these years. Remember when we got married and we made a vow that if we ever wanted to cheat on one another we'd get a divorce first?" She looked down at the diamond solitare on her left hand.

"Well, I've kept my part of the vow, no matter what you might think, even though I strongly doubt you've kept yours." He turned his eyes to avoid her direct gaze. She stopped and when he looked back at her, she continued. Her tone was even, solemn.

"Other men are beginning to appeal to me now, and I'm leaving you."

He started to rise from his chair.

"Oh, that's not the only reason," she said and put a hand up and he slumped back into his chair.

"It's not the only reason, but it's a big part of it."

"I don't believe you!" he responded angrily. "Who is it?!"

"You," she said evenly. "It's you. That makes you mad because, if there was someone else you could blame, it would make my leaving easier for you. Easier for you to explain to your friends. Well, it's you, it's us. I don't want to be with you any more. I don't like you any more. Sure, I love you, and probably always will love you to some extent. But I don't like you, and I haven't liked you for a long time. So, you're the reason I'm leaving. Only you."

She sensed the intense rage within him. She knew this dialogue was necessary. Whether he was understanding her words and believing her was another matter.

"You can't leave."

"Tell me why not."

"Because I love you."

"Love is a neurosis. Tell me something you like about me."

He was silent. They stared at each other. No matter what he said, what arguments he might have, she was getting out.

"Okay, let's see if we've got anything we can start with and build upon. Do you like the way I look?"

"No."

"Do you like the way I dress?"

"No."

"Do you like my job?" Whenever he complained about her job, the travel it required, the long hours, she volunteered to get into some other work that was less demanding but he said she couldn't quit. He was accustomed to the money she brought home, the car, the perks.

"No."

"Do you like the way I keep house?" She readily admitted to being a lousy housekeeper. She wouldn't deny him that criticism.

"No."

"Do you like the way I cook?"

"No."

"Do you like to make love to me?"

He was silent. That answer was simple. For years she'd had to beg him to make love to her. He acted as though it was a major chore, servicing her once or twice a year at best. She knew, as most wives know, there were other women and it angered her all the more that she had to beg. Particularly when there were so many men, so many interesting, intelligent men who displayed interest in being around her socially.

She could feel the anger rising, knotting in her chest, spreading its tentacles into her brain. She pushed against it. This was no time for emotion to overrule logic. She was almost out. This was merely cleanup time.

"You can't go," he said softly. "You need me."

"No, you need me. You once told me that a salesman's best asset was his patter, his words, his line. Call it what you want, but you told me yourself that salesmen are not to be believed. And right now I don't believe you." When he worked, he sold used cars. When he worked.

"Then you're not willing to even try to work it out?"

"I've been trying for fourteen years! Now I'm through trying! I'm leaving. There's nothing left to talk about. I asked you to name just one thing you liked about me and you couldn't think of even one small insignificant thing you liked. Not one! Not that it would have mattered at this point. I've given it my utmost best. I'm drained, empty, there's nothing left. I don't want to stay with you any longer."

She kept her eyes locked to his as she talked. His eyes showed no emotion, they were cold, passionless. She wondered if he would go into the garage, load one of his guns, come back into the house and blow her brains out. It was a strong possibility.

"So when are you leaving?"

"I'm going to look for an apartment this weekend."

"You won't go for counseling with me?"

Perhaps he felt he and the good doctor could double-team her.

"No." She'd spent an expensive fifty-minute hour with their counselor three weeks earlier. She asked him what she should do.

"You'll make the right decision," was his response. He never answered her questions directly and sometimes it angered her because she wanted him to share the burden of a bad decision. She wanted him to earn his money.

"You won't even give it one chance?"

"It's a waste of money and my time. You don't seem to understand. I'm through. Nothing you have to say will change the way I feel."

"At least promise me you won't go looking for an apartment for a couple weeks."

"Why?"

"Because if you go looking, you'll find one, and then it'll be too late for you to turn back."

"You're still not listening. It's over."

"Then at least make me a promise."

"A promise about what?"

"Promise you'll find a place as far away as possible so we won't be running into each other."

"That's no problem," she said. "I'll get as far away as I can without leaving my job or the state. Is that far enough?"

"Yes. But, one more thing."

"What?"

"You're not taking anything with you except your clothes."

"Fine." She was prepared to walk out with nothing.

"You try to get the house, the other property, the cars, anything, I'll fight you. It won't matter to me if attorneys get it all, I'll make sure you get nothing."

She knew this was his final bluff, his supposed ace in the hole. He thought she'd stay for the possessions they'd accumulated through the years. He considered possessions to be important, she didn't. It was another of their basic differences.

"I'll sign everything over to you, no problem."

"The dog and the cat stay."

She wanted to laugh at the absurdity of his statement. And she wanted to cry because her pets had been the only loving creatures she'd been around for a long time.

"They stay."

"You'll pay for the attorney."

"I will."

"Another thing."

"Now what?"

"I don't want the papers served at my office. I'll pick them up."

"Fine."

It was amazing to her. It was as though he'd already known, that he'd thought the whole thing through. Or maybe all along he'd been expecting her to leave and he'd been coached by his therapy group so her leaving would be profitable and easy for him. As far as not having him served at his office, she believed he made the request since his co-workers probably didn't know he was married.

"Are you absolutely sure you know what you're doing? There's no turning back, you know."

"I'm absolutely sure, and, yes, I know."

He got up from his chair, walked to the front door, opened it. He turned back to face her.

"I do love you."

"Yes, I'm sure. And I love you," she replied softly and then paused. "But it's over."

He turned, walked outside, closed the door. She heard his car door slam, the engine rev. And then he was gone.

Karen found a rental condo the next weekend, far across town, in a trendy complex for working professionals who either were divorced, or would be soon. The rent was high but it was the beginning of her new life and she didn't plan to scrimp on any part of it. A week later she was living in her condo and three days later she had her attorney file for the divorce.

"How long have you been separated?" he asked.

"I moved out last Friday."

"You can't file that quickly! It just isn't done!"

"File it."

"You can't be sure! It's too soon, you might change your mind!" A fatherly type in his mid-sixties, he believed marriage and family came before all else.

"I won't change my mind. Why does everyone think I don't know my own mind? I won't back out! Just get the paperwork done so I can get on with my life." She was irritated. "Incidentally, he gets everything."

"What?! This is a community property state. You're entitled to a fifty-fifty split."

"No. He gets everything."

"I won't do it. It's unfair to you."

"Fine. Someone else will do it, maybe not as good as you and maybe they won't be looking out for my welfare like you are, but they'll take my money anyway."

"Are you certain this is what you want?" There was disappointment in his voice, but resignation also.

"Look, it was because of me, my hard work, my salary, that we got the house, the rental property, the cars, the nice furnishings, all of it. Now, so I won't feel guilty about leaving him to fend for himself for the first time in his adult life, I'm giving it all to him. What he does with it is up to him. But he's not going to be able to say that I threw him out, that I caused his downfall. There's nothing there I want. Not the memories, not the guilt, nothing. He gets it all!"

"Okay, I'll draw up the papers if you're quite sure."

"I am. Oh, one more thing. He wants to pick the papers up here, he doesn't want them served."

"I'll call you when they're ready and we'll set up an appointment."

"Fine. And fast, okay? I need this to be over."

"What grounds do I use?"

"The standard. Irreconcilable differences. He's agreeing to the divorce, he's not getting an attorney." She didn't tell him it was because he was too cheap to pay for an attorney. That seemed inconsequential now.

A week later, when they met in her attorney's office, he was cold and distant. He didn't read the papers her attorney handed to him but instead stared past her at the wall.

Quit claim deeds had been drawn up on their properties and she signed them all. Her attorney explained there'd be a charge for the doc stamps for deed recording.

"How much?" Tommy demanded.

Her attorney turned toward her and she could almost read his thoughts. Is he serious? You're turning over thousands of dollars worth of property to him without a fight and he wants to know how much the doc stamps are going to cost him?

"How much?!" he demanded irritably.

Karen's attorney turned to his secretary and asked her to get the figures. She came back into the office. "No more than fifty dollars."

Tommy was pursing his lips, working his mouth, a habit she'd grown to loathe.

"Look, I'll pay for the damn stamps!" she shouted. "Add it to my bill!"

Her attorney shook his head then stood up to indicate the appointment was over. Tommy made a quick exit.

Karen turned to her attorney. "Do you really need a list of reasons why I want a divorce?"

"No," he said. "I'll push this through as fast as I can. You'll be seeing a magistrate and he might give you some problems about doing this so quickly without a trial separation. You be as convincing with him as you have been with me, and maybe he'll grant the divorce without any strings or conditions."

The magistrate was another fatherly type who wouldn't hear of her giving everything away after so many years of marriage.

"Sir," she stated emphatically. "I, by hard work, caused the accumulation of the majority of those possessions. And, I, by more hard work, will acquire more possessions. What I'm asking of you is that you allow me my freedom to enjoy life."

"Are you certain this is what you want?" It was the most annoying question people were asking her.

"Absolutely!"

"Have you received counseling?"

"Yes, sir."

"Joint counseling?"

"He's in therapy, and has been for the past ten years. We've been counseled by the same doctor, although not at the same time."

"And, your doctor, what did he say about this?"

"He told me I would make the right decision. This is my decision."

"To give up everything."

"To give up possessions. I can always buy more possessions. I can't buy freedom. I'm asking you to give me my freedom."

"You won't change your mind? You won't seek additional counseling?"

"No, sir. There's no need."

"Then I grant your request, and best of luck to you, young lady."

She breathed deeply. Free. Really, truly free. She smiled for the first time in a long, long time.

Karen filled her non-working hours with university courses, did volunteer work, and indulged herself by taking art classes. When she felt confident enough about her watercolors to display them at local art shows, a new chapter began, and it was then that Marcella entered her life.

She had no intention of getting married again. Once was more than enough. It was a surprise, a shock, a joyous occasion when she met, fell in love with, and then married Charles Bryce, a wealthy importer-exporter.

Charles' sudden death so soon after their marriage plunged her into the depths of depression.

She had no intentions of ever falling in love again.

DEATH IN THE MORNING

Herbert reached over to draw Sandra to him. It was an unexpected bonus to wake up and find her still in his bed. She normally waited until she heard his loud snores then retired to her suite of rooms where she took a long cleansing bath before sleeping.

Herbert's hand touched Sandra's naked arm. He was still groggy with sleep and the memory of last night's rough passion was fresh in his thoughts. The unusual clamminess of her skin took a few seconds to register and then he bolted out of bed.

The ambulance took Sandra's body to Centro Asturiano Hospital where an autopsy was performed. The mixture of cocaine, valium, alcohol and numerous barbiturates was easy enough to find, and, while each was not present in enough quantity to be lethal by itself, the pathology report indicated the combination had, indeed, caused her death.

The small amount of chemical that led to her death went undetected.

Herbert was aware of Sandra's cocaine habit and also her heavy use of barbiturates though he deliberately chose to play ignorant. He made a point of turning to Marcella for help. Marcella, after careful thought, told him about Sandra's involvement with Greg White. With Marcella as the informant, Herbert took appropriate action to save face as the husband wronged.

The State's Attorney quickly indicted White on manslaughter and drug trafficking charges. His trial was equally swift and he found himself serving twenty years to life in Raiford where his blond hair and trim tanned body made him popular among the inmates.

Sandra's father left town as quietly as he had arrived.

Sandra was entombed in the Bianci family's mausoleum at Myrtle Hill Cemetery next to Herbert's first wife. The 65-carat diamond necklace with its huge cabochon sapphire pendant, Herbert's gift to Sandra their last night together, was placed in his safety deposit box.

And, at Marcella's luncheons, Sandra's place was set as usual.

FOOD FOR THOUGHT

"Death? I don't believe in it in the traditional sense," said Bobbi.

It had been six weeks since Sandra's death and Marcella's group was lunching again in the Garden Room. While they always met for lunch, the lunch hour most times went far into the afternoon and re-sembled an informal business meeting more than a women's social.

Karen, Bobbi, Cissy and Candy regularly attended Marcella's luncheons. Sandra's place was always set. Marcella thought it a nice a touch, a macabre reminder of good triumphing over evil.

"And what sense do you believe in?" smirked Cissy. She had little tolerance for Bobbi, the blue-blooded heiress to whom everything came so easily.

"I shouldn't have opened my mouth," said Bobbi meekly.

"No, do continue, dear," Marcella prodded as she buttered a croissant.

"I follow the belief that the universe is composed of energy. How it started, that I can't comprehend. Logic says everything must have a beginning so we have the chicken and the egg debate." Bobbi paused.

"Oh, Christ!" exclaimed Cissy. "I heard all this in freshman philosophy."

Marcella gave Cissy a hard stare then turned to smile at Bobbi. "You have my interest, dear, please continue."

"I really don't think my views are good luncheon listening," replied Bobbi.

"Please, I'd like to hear more," said Karen.

"So would I," agreed Candy, her blue eyes sparkling.

"Okay, you asked for it, boring theory and all," laughed Bobbi. She settled back in her chair and steepled her fingers in front of her.

"Basically, we have a big bang to start it all, spreading little energy particles throughout the universe, world, whatever. A creature is born, an energy particle has a home. A creature dies, the energy particle leaves that home and finds another."

"Are you calling these energy particles the soul?" asked Karen.

"For want of a better term, soul will do," replied Bobbi.

"So you're saying Sandra's energy went out of her body and into someone—"

"Or something else," Bobbi finished Candy's question.

"Which could explain reincarnation quite nicely," Marcella mused.

"Yes, it could. And for me it's a pleasant thought, an easier way to think of death rather than one minute you're here and the next minute you're erased, a nothing, a pile of ashes or whatever."

"And just what do your energy particles inhabit?" asked Cissy.

"All life forms," responded Bobbi.

"So our dear departed Sandra could have popped back in the body of — let's say for descriptive purposes — a slug?"

"Cissy!" cried Candy. "That's cruel! Be kind with thoughts of the dead!"

"Hey, I'm not the one who came up with this crazy theory. Talk to the lady over there," Cissy pointed a porcelain fingernail at Bobbi.

"Bobbi, is that what you believe?" asked Candy incredulously.

"In the broadest sense of terms, I suppose so. But, because memory — and this again is my own personal belief — remains with the body, the energy spark would be nothing more than a propellant, a fuel, for the next form it inhabited. Like taking a battery out of a flashlight and putting it into a calculator. Of course, there's always the possibility the energy spark, or particle would unite with the main energy source and it would then lose any individual identity."

"What a bunch of bull!" snapped Cissy. "I suppose you're now going to tell us this main energy source is God."

"Everyone is entitled to their own opinions, Cissy," scolded Candy.

"Actually, Cissy, that's exactly what I believe."

"Why, Bobbi," exclaimed Marcella. "That's really quite a pleasant theory. That would mean we're all a part of God."

"Yes, if you want to put a name to the energy source, 'God' is as good a name as any. If you think it out long enough, there's no conflict with the Bible's version of creation, nor does it conflict with the other major religions. Not if you consider happenings in their broadest interpretations, which is not a new concept. There are teachings going back through the centuries along parallel thoughts."

"You're incredible," said Cissy, her voice dripping with sarcasm. "In less than an hour you've turned God into nothing more than an electrical power plant, suggested that Sandra has been reborn in the body of a slug, and equated the Bible, Torah, Koran and every other religious work with travelogues and philosophy books!"

"Cissy, that—"

"It's okay, Marcella, I'm a big girl, I can defend myself. You remember I was reluctant to continue this discussion."

"I think," said Karen. "That is an interesting concept and I would like to pursue it with you whenever you've got some free time. And, Cissy, Bobbi has just been stating some of the beliefs of some of the greatest minds of history. Bobbi? Will you have time sometime soon?"

"Tomorrow evening?" asked Bobbi, relieved to have a comrade in Karen. She respected Karen's opinions.

"Perfect. I'll have Mary put together one of her gourmet wonders and you and Chris can plan on dinner around seven."

"Chris is going out of town—"

"Even better! That'll mean more of Mary's goodies for us while we spend some time exploring your ideas."

"You two are enough to make me want to puke. I personally will be just as happy to die and stay dead, thank you, rather than pop up in some lesser life form," sniffed Cissy.

"Aw, come on, Cissy, I can picture you as, oh, maybe a fox," laughed Candy.

"How about a head of lettuce?" ventured Karen.

"No, no!" exclaimed Marcella. "Cissy is more the man-eater type." She gave a throaty laugh and raised her wine glass in a mock salute to Cissy.

"A panther!" squealed Candy getting into the spirit of the banter.

"Or a tiger. Maybe a leopard." Candy looked at Marcella and grinned. She knew better than anyone how much and why Marcella despised Cissy.

"Why not a Venus fly trap?" asked Karen.

"Or a black widow, the spider, of course," howled Candy.

"I hate all of you!" screamed Cissy as she pushed her chair away from the table. "I've got better things to do with my time than spend it with a washed-up society bitch, her whore social secretary, and a couple rich-bitch flakes!"

"Oh, my, do you think we went too far?" asked Marcella as Cissy stormed out of the restaurant. She held her wine glass up for the waiter to refill.

"No, I think we actually could have gone much further," answered Karen.

"Definitely," said Candy.

"I picture her in her next life as a scorpion," replied Bobbi.

"Serve her right to be a slug," countered Candy.

"Girls, girls, girls," chided Marcella. "Be nice. We'd all feel badly if something happened to Cissy, wouldn't we?"

"I've dominated our conversation so far. What I'd like to know, Candy, is how your great love affair is coming along," said Bobbi.

"We're getting married," said Candy.

There were squeals of delight from around the table. It was a lot different than the conversation months before when she'd told everyone she was giving up men.

"You've what!?" screeched Marcella. "Next we'll hear the earth has stopped rotating! It's not natural!"

"Aren't you exaggerating just a bit?" asked Karen.

"Perhaps a wee bit, but, come on, Candy, you can't be serious."

"Oh, I am," replied Candy softly. "Once I learned that I myself could control and produce pleasure no man ever could, I felt dirty and ashamed for all the men—"

"Maybe you're over-reacting?" asked Bobbi.

"Look, I've told you about all the men I've slept with, even the group sex and some pretty kinky stuff. I thought I was right in what I was doing. You know, like it was natural. I honestly believed it. And then..."

What?" Bobbi prompted.

"I was trying with all those men to find something that they couldn't provide. And then I found I had the answers myself." Candy looked at Marcella and gave a shy smile.

"Now, look, honey, I didn't mean for you to cut men out of your life entirely," said Marcella.

"What in heaven's name did you do, Marcella?"

Marcella looked at Candy. "I suggested she investigate the pleasures of single sex."

"Masturbation?!" Bobbi whispered.

Candy's cheeks flushed bright red.

"Hey, it's not a closet activity, though you won't find too many people openly advocating the practice or admitting that they indulge," replied Bobbi.

"Then you don't think I was crazy for preferring to stay at home alone?" Candy asked.

"You're not crazy. If the truth was known, I'd wager more than a few of the sophisticated 'Cosmo girls' are spending a great deal of solo time with their vibrators. But any behavior that becomes compulsive, or all-consuming to the exclusion of other activities, could bear a hard look," said Karen.

"Plain English?" asked Candy.

"Don't give up men altogether," said Bobbi.

"Thanks," Candy had said. "But I'm going to be very, very choosy from now on."

And along came Jimmy.

Afterlife

"You're talking about the anti-matter theory of Krishna, aren't you?"

Karen and Bobbi finished dinner and were having after dinner drinks in the spacious, pastel living room of Karen's home. The furnishings were simplistic but well appointed, priceless paintings hung on the walls and equally priceless statuary perched on marble tables and atop ebony shelves.

Karen's second husband, having made a huge fortune in the import-export business, indulged Karen's desire to collect fine art. After his untimely death, she continued her collection.

"Maybe some parts," Bobbi responded. "I studied yoga, and when Chris and I were in one of our more spiritual periods, we studied under a Krishna swami. But I'm not holding to out-of-body space travel at will which is part of the Krishna teaching."

"Oh, that could save our country a lot of money if it worked," laughed Karen. "Think of the millions or billions we could save in space shuttle costs."

"Honestly, do you think this is silly?"

"Heavens, no!" exclaimed Karen. "I have beliefs very much like your own, that's why I wanted us to talk without distractions."

"You mean Cissy," said Bobbi.

"Yes. She can get quite vindictive."

"I suppose she has good reasons sometimes."

"Bobbi, I think you're too good-natured."

"I just believe everyone has reasons for what they do. And I don't expect others to answer to me for their actions."

"Live and let live?" Karen smiled.

"Something like that."

"Does it have anything to do with your energy theory?"

"I suppose it does. I mean, if a person is a real pain to someone else, and then they die and their spark goes into someone else who has to deal with, or be dealt with, by precedents or prejudices set by the other person, well, it gets complicated to explain—"

"You're doing very well, or maybe it's the wine. I do understand what you're saying, and, you know, I think you've got a good point." Karen reached for the baccarat crystal decanter to refill their glasses.

"Karen, you've had a lot of negatives in your life. You've talked vaguely about your first husband and you've said that was a bad experience. When Charles died it floored us all, and you seemed wiped out. It took a lot of personal strength to pull back into reality," Bobbi paused, wondering if she'd spoken too much. "I'm sorry; I wouldn't have mentioned it—"

"My dear, I still cry myself to sleep some nights so let's not try to pretend it didn't happen just so I won't be hurt, okay?"

"Where do you get your strength?" asked Bobbi.

"The same place you get yours," replied Karen.

Bobbi looked at her quizzically.

"From inside," said Karen as she tapped a finger to her temple.

"Oh."

"Bobbi, you give everyone more chances than they deserve. You don't get mad when you've been slapped; you don't try to get even when most people would. Why not? What is there inside you that makes you forgive, turn the other cheek?"

"You're making me out to be a saint."

"I don't know anyone who fits the bill any closer. And Chris, he's the same way."

"Yeah, he is a pretty wonderful guy at that," smiled Bobbi.

"So, while we're busy opening up, how come you turn everything into lemonade all the time?"

"Karen, my parents were killed when I was very young. My paternal aunt and uncle took me into their home and made me feel like I was a normal, regular, necessary part of their family. They could have turned their backs, but they didn't. They were older people with grown children and yet they willingly accepted the burden of raising me."

"You consider yourself a burden?"

"Ah, going to play analyst with me, doctor?"

"Sorry."

"So maybe I do — or did. And so maybe I'm thankful every day that two such wonderful people took me in without hesitation and sacrificed the years they could have been traveling, enjoying life, just the two of them. They were unique, special."

"I'm certain they were. And I've no doubt they didn't hesitate even a second when you needed a home. I'll bet they're immensely proud of you."

"They died five years ago in a plane crash." Tears welled up in Bobbi's eyes.

"I'm sorry."

"But, that's where the energy or anti-matter theory helps. I can accept their deaths and the deaths of others if there's a chance they aren't really dead in spirit — that's what counts —spirit."

Her acceptance of death and the energy transfer theory only held so much credence. She couldn't see or feel or talk to anyone who had died and been transferred. It was crazy. Even crazier were the days when she didn't want to spray bugs or pull up weeds, thinking she was destroying a viable life.

"Karen," whispered Bobbi. "Why don't we set up an anti-matter foundation? I'll pull some money out of my trust fund, you match it, and we'll hire experts, do extensive research, prove it or disprove it once and for all."

Karen raised her head and stared at Bobbi.

"You know, that's one superb idea," declared Karen. "And it'll get me off dead-center."

"So, what'll we call our foundation?"

"Energy Flow Foundation?" suggested Karen.

"Spark—" started Bobbi.

"—of Life! That's perfect! The Spark of Life Foundation! Perfect! I love it! How about it?" Karen clapped her hands with enthusiasm.

"Spark of Life Foundation?" mused Bobbi. "It does have a ring to it, doesn't it?"

"I like it. I really do," said Karen.

"Okay, Spark of Life it is," agreed Bobbi. "So shall we get our attorneys working on the papers in the morning?"

"I'm ready," answered Karen.

They toasted themselves and their new foundation.

It could have been an interesting proposition if events had not conspired to push the foundation into oblivion before it could begin.

EXIT ED

Karen received the frantic call from Marcella just after Bobbi left her house.

"It's Ed," Marcella sobbed. "You've got to come help me; you'll know what to do."

"Please, Marcie," said Karen. "Please tell me what's wrong."

"He's dead," cried Marcella. "My wonderful Ed is dead!"

Ed's death from a massive stroke stunned the business community and appeared to devastate Marcella. Later, after the funeral, at the reading of Ed's will, Marcella learned the extent of Cissy's control over Ed and Grand Enterprises.

To Marcella, Ed left his portion of their jointly-owned properties along with nine percent interest in Grand Enterprises, the corporation Marcella inherited at her father's death.

To Cissy, Ed left a cash settlement of $500,000 along with his remaining forty-percent interest in Grand Enterprises. Cissy was now quite wealthy.

Shock waves went through Marcella's circle of friends. It had been Marcella's decision to transfer the forty-nine percent ownership of Grand Enterprises to Ed. She believed he would have a stronger incentive to keep the business growing if he experienced a direct benefit. She retained the controlling fifty-one percent.

Marcella had been unaware of recent changes Ed had made in his will, adding the bequests to Cissy. It had been a blackmail move he was forced into but one he hadn't intended on fulfilling. He intended to amend his will, removing her from it, as soon as she aborted his child. It was something about which Marcella could not have known.

Cissy didn't gloat about her new status but neither did she shy away from taking over the day-to-day operation of the business. It was apparent to Marcella that Cissy knew the business better than anyone else and Marcella allowed her to continue. If the business began showing a decline, Marcella was prepared to take action.

Herbert and Marcella had long been involved as silent partners in each other's business ventures. Herbert was Marcella's advisor, and he was quietly monitoring the books to prevent any nasty surprises should Cissy plan a takeover.

After Ed's death, Marcella leaned on Herbert for emotional support. It was more a ploy than a real need. When Herbert returned from Las Vegas with his young wife in tow, Marcella felt betrayed. Herbert was the one man she thought had more sense than to fall for some hot young bimbo.

With Ed and Sandra permanently out of the way, and Herbert thoroughly disenchanted with the cards dealt him in his personal life, it was time for Marcella to make her move.

Quiet dinners at home, pleasant reminiscing over drinks paved the way for more intimate encounters until one evening it was instinctive that they should spend the night together in Marcella's massive bed.

For Marcella it was not a noteworthy event. For Herbert, who had gone without the earthy warmth of a sturdy woman for so long, and who appreciated Marcella's lusty sexual appetite, it was one of the most satisfying nights of his life.

Their nights together became more frequent and it was Herbert who, after a sumptuous dinner of veal scaloppini and linguine with garlic butter, suggested they merge all their assets.

"Herbert, are you proposing?"

"Yes, my dear, I believe I am."

"Well, then, my loving Herbert," crooned Marcella. "I accept."

Their quiet marriage two weeks later surprised no one. That it was so soon after Ed's and Sandra's deaths was of no major consequence.

After a honeymoon cruise on the QE II, they placed both their homes on the market and bought a two-story penthouse atop the Bayshore Towers overlooking Tampa Bay. Marcella didn't want to live in Herbert's huge mansion with its unpleasant memories and Sandra's gauche decorating. When Herbert suggested they live in her huge home Marcella refused saying she wanted them to have a fresh start.

Herbert's children were apprehensive about their father's marriage, fearing their inheritances would suffer. To mollify their fears, Herbert created trust funds for each.

The business ownerships were covered in their new wills, with Herbert's complete control going to Marcella should he predecease her, hers going to him should she predecease him. Herbert's children and grandchildren were to share equally should Marcella and Herbert die at the same time. Herbert's will was a mere formality; he had business partners who would take control at his death — from among them a don would be chosen to succeed him.

Marcella was back in control — or so she thought.

Lunch At Marcella's

"It's just so wonderful to have a man around the house again," Marcella crooned.

Lunch was being served by Marcella's black maid, one of two servants who lived in separate quarters in the sumptuous penthouse.

"It's been such an incredibly sad year," mused Karen as she gazed out the balcony windows to the Bay.

"I just don't believe it. Sandra. And then Ed," said Bobbi.

"Lots of little energy sparks flying around looking for new homes, huh?" Cissy asked spitefully.

"Cissy, you're a guest in my home!"

"Well, excuse me, Marcella. So nice you don't have any bad feelings about your husband's death. There are some of us—"

"For crying out loud, Cissy!" Candy shouted. She hated Cissy for causing Marcella so much pain.

"My love for Ed was a private matter," said Marcella as tears came to her eyes.

"Unlike my public love for him?" asked Cissy scornfully.

"That's it," said Bobbi. "There's been enough sniping for me for one day. Marcella, thanks for the meal. Sorry I have to run but something just came up."

"Bobbi, stay seated!" Marcella commanded. "Cissy, you need to go."

"Sure, no problem," Cissy said as she threw her napkin on her plate. "Marcella, you may want to pretend Ed loved you, but that's a fairy tale you tell yourself and your cronies. Everybody here knows he loved me and that he was going to leave you. His will is proof and you know it!"

"You bitch, get out!" Marcella shrieked.

"With pleasure. Do have a good afternoon, ladies, and I use the term very loosely," Cissy said as she left.

"Why can I never find even one good thing about that woman?" asked Bobbi.

"If you do," replied Karen, "be sure and share it with us. Marcella, why do you put up with her?"

"Ed was quite fond of her, you know," Marcella replied as if in a daze.

Candy stabbed at her salad.

CLOSING TIME

The spa attendant was making a final check before closing when she saw something large and bright pink at the bottom of the whirlpool.

It was hours later before she was calm enough to tell the police what little she could remember prior to her discovery of the body in the whirlpool. She watched the last stragglers leave just before ten then spent forty or fifty minutes finishing paperwork in her office before making her rounds, returned various pieces of exercise equipment to their proper places, shutting off the sauna, the steam room, the whirlpool.

Yes, it was possible someone had been overlooked when she locked the front doors. It wouldn't be the first time a member had been in a dressing room at closing time.

Cissy was wearing a shocking pink sweat suit when her body was retrieved from the whirlpool. When she was tagged and placed in cold storage at the morgue, the sweat suit was replaced by a threadbare white sheet.

She was the most attractive guest the morgue had received in months and she proved popular among the night attendants. Who would know? Who would care? Cissy certainly would never tell. It was almost like a farewell party for her — the kind she had given for so many of her lovers. She might have enjoyed the festivities had she been alive.

It was mid-morning when the young medical examiner pulled the sheet back from her face, shook his head and slowly pulled the sheet from her body. The older man across the table from him sighed loudly.

"She's a beauty, isn't she?" asked the older man.

"Yeah, a pity we always get them when they're stiff and cold," replied the younger man.

The older man sighed again.

"Well, shall we find out why she won't be dancing any more?" He turned on the recorder, picked up a scalpel and made the first cut.

The autopsy took two hours and twenty minutes. Both men knew more about Cissy after that length of time than anyone else had known in her entire lifetime. She had excellent muscle tone and minimal excess body fat. She'd had an appendectomy when she was a child, several abortions and a recent tubal ligation. Her organs were of average size and weight. Her lungs had traces of chlorinated water which matched samples taken from the whirlpool. Tissue samples were taken for further study.

"Uh, oh, take a look at this," said the older man as he motioned the younger M.E. to the microscope.

"That's funny," murmured the younger man as he studied the slide. "She didn't strike me as your typical druggie type."

"Don't let it get you down. The more time you spend around here, the less you'll be surprised by anything you find."

"So she OD's and drowns as a result?"

"That's the way it looks to me. So what's your cause of death for the death certificate?"

"Accidental drowning."

"You're catching on," replied the older man as he rubbed his eyes and then reached for the bottle marked "Formaldehyde" and put it up to his mouth. The cheap vodka burned his throat. His was the kind of job that required periodic alcohol breaks to make it to quitting time.

Detective Work

Bobbi pressed against the side of the building as she inched her way toward the barbed wire fence surrounding the equipment yard. She avoided the lighted areas and looked for trip wires or other security devices that might warn the building's occupants of her presence. She kept a tight grip on her Smith & Wesson .38 and as she inched along she prayed that she wouldn't have to use the gun — not that she couldn't, and not that she wouldn't.

The call had come for Chris six hours earlier.

"Let me speak to Christopher Walker," the man demanded.

Bobbi didn't like his tone of voice and she asked who was calling.

"If he's there, let me speak to him. If he's not there, then forget it," the man responded coldly.

Chris took the phone from Bobbi and gave a terse, "Yes?" He listened and frowned.

"Are you absolutely certain?" he asked the caller.

"Of course I am!" he exclaimed to the caller's response. "Right now! Just give me the directions," he said excitedly and motioned to Bobbi to bring him paper and pencil. He scribbled an address and hung up the phone.

"Holy shit!" he exclaimed as he threw the pencil down.

"What is it? And who was that?" asked Bobbi.

"That was Mark Garrett—"

"*The* Mark Garrett?" asked Bobbi. Garrett was big time trouble.

"The one and the same," said Chris.

"He wanted to know if I was interested in getting solid evidence against the company that's been dumping toxic waste into our water supply."

"What?!"

"He claims he can show me the dumping site, and I can watch the trucks come and go. I can get pictures, talk to some of the workers."

"That doesn't sound like Garrett. Why would he get involved, and why is he all of a sudden turning good guy —assuming he is?" Bobbi had researched Garrett's background thoroughly when she and Chris first got involved in the fight to stop toxic pollution of the area's major water sources. Mark Garrett was owner of a borrow pit and his activities had gotten him a lion's share of press coverage for several months, then he went to jail on what he claimed were trumped up charges, and it took the majority of his savings to grease enough political palms to get him out of jail.

"Look, the man has an ax to grind. He says he was set up, that he can prove it. He just doesn't want anyone to know he's the one blowing the whistle. He's been seeing my name in the newspapers lately, and figures that if I blow the whistle someone will listen." Chris shrugged his shoulders.

"This may be a wild goose chase, but I have to go after it. He's waiting for me now. I want you to call Arnie, tell him to go to Garrett's borrow pit on Bayfront Road. Garrett told me to come alone, and that's what I'm going to do, but if Arnie wants the exclusive, if there is one, he can meet me."

Chris ran a hand through his thick blond hair in a futile attempt to tame it, gave Bobbi a quick kiss on the forehead, picked up his car keys and headed out the door.

"This shouldn't take too long."

Bobbi dialed Arnie's home number. Arnie answered on the second ring.

"He's doing what?" he shouted after Bobbi relayed Chris' message. "He could get himself killed!"

"Don't you think you're exaggerating a bit?" asked Bobbi, though instinct told her he probably wasn't.

"Goddamnit! Garrett's a convicted felon. Even if he's telling the truth don't you know that whenever there's something this big at stake people have been known to disappear? Goddamnit! I'm on my way!"

The connection broke and Bobbi suspected Arnie had slammed the phone down.

Arnie was a reporter for the *Times*, somewhat eccentric, a little offbeat, an outdated hippie in Chris' evaluation, but he wasn't afraid to take chances to get a headline. His investigative tactics had landed him in the hospital several times. Once, when he was beaten and dumped in the Everglades, he crawled through miles of swamp until he reached "Alligator Alley," where he was found by a carload of tourists. It had been a botched job — he wasn't supposed to survive. He made his deadline and blew apart a contracting scam in South Florida.

Bobbi could see a number of huge dump trucks and garbage trucks in the distance, far behind the tall security fence with its barbed wire top. Trucks were being stopped at the guard gate and checked by two armed, unsmiling private cops. They looked like ex Viet vets, the kind who liked to carry guns but couldn't pass the psychological tests for regular police work.

The kind who were dangerous because they took their jobs too seriously.

The small block office sat just to the front and side of the security gate. The office was dark so it didn't seem likely that Chris and Arnie were still there — if that had been their starting point.

She didn't know what to do or where to go for help. The little bit of information Arnie gave her before he rushed out to meet Chris had been just enough to make her realize there was no one within the local police or local government who would be safe to go to for help. If it indeed was the multi-million dollar scam that Arnie believed was going on, it meant there were a lot of judges, police, and government officials on the take. That information would be fine if they could be sure who the corrupt officials were — but they couldn't.

"Lambs into the wolves' den," was the phrase Arnie used when Chris and Bobbi talked about going public with the dumping at the borrow pit.

The revolver was a heavy weight in her hand and she realized she was gripping the gun much tighter than necessary. She loosened her grip, gave her arm a slight shake, and took a couple deep breaths. Okay, hot shot, she thought, don't screw up now.

Bobbi crept closer to the edge of the building and opened her mouth to scream as two figures came at her from around the corner. She raised the gun and before she could take aim Chris grabbed her wrist, yanked the gun from her hand, and, at the same time, Arnie put his meaty hand over her mouth. Bobbi slumped forward into Chris' arms.

"Do you know how close you came to being shot?!" hissed Bobbi when Arnie pulled his hand from over her mouth. She glowered at both of them.

"No time for niceties, guys," whispered Arnie. "Let's get the hell out of here before we're spotted."

They stayed in the shadows and worked their way to where Bobbi had parked her car off the road, a quarter mile from the entrance to the borrow pit. Bobbi unlocked the Porsche Targa, Chris climbed into the passenger seat, and Arnie folded himself into the jump seat. Bobbi started the car then turned to look at both men.

"Well?"

"Well, what?" responded Chris and Arnie in unison.

"Well, for chrissakes I've been going out of my mind worrying so what is going on and where are your cars and where am I going?!"

"One thing at a time and slow down," said Chris as he placed a hand on Bobbi's shoulder and began a slow kneading massage.

"We're alright, first of all, as you can plainly see. Secondly, both our cars are at Garrett's house, which, for your information, is in the direction you're headed."

"And thirdly," said Arnie in his booming voice. "We've got ourselves one monumental ass-kicking story on our hands!"

"So tell me," demanded Bobbi.

"In due course, little girl," said Chris. "Take a right at that next intersection. You can let us off, we'll walk the rest of the way. No need to disturb the Garrett family unnecessarily this late at night. We'll meet you back at the house and tell you the whole—"

"Monumentally big—" interjected Arnie.

"Story," finished Chris.

Bobbi made the turn, stopped her car and watched as Chris and Arnie walked down the tree-lined street. An imposing two-story wooden house was visible in the distance. Only one upstairs light was on. The yard was unlighted.

Bobbi had drinks mixed and ready when Chris and Arnie walked through the door. "Now. Sit. Speak." she commanded as the men took their drinks and headed for the den.

"Okay, this is the way it plays," started Arnie. "And right now we're not sure where to go with it or how to protect ourselves when we do get enough facts to back up the stories we've heard tonight." He took a sip of the bloody mary and grimaced.

"Carried away with the hot sauce, huh?"

"That's for putting me through it tonight," said Bobbi with a grin.

"Anyway, according to Garrett — and he's got us sworn to secrecy about his part in this — we've got graft at every level of government all the way up to Washington. There's a judge, two councilmen, those are small potatoes, then a senator and a congressman, and of course their political cronies. The chemical plant has been dumping some nasty shit in the pit, according to Garrett. And that's only the tip of the iceberg scam that's taking place. Assuming Garrett is telling us the truth."

"The million dollar assumption," responded Chris.

"According to Garrett, and he says he can show us the trucks, give us times and dates, we take pictures for solid evidence, et cetera, et cetera, the pits have become a major dumping ground for a conglomeration of toxic waste producers. He says there's a Watergate-type cover-up taking place to protect the asses of all the bigwigs on the take. They can sacrifice a few sheep if necessary to save themselves."

"But what can we do?" asked Bobbi.

"Now that's the million dollar question," said Arnie. "Garrett says the dumping going on at his place is no worse than what's happening at other sites in the area. He says he has copies of tests done by an independent lab — an out-of-state lab, by the way. I mean this guy is running scared and if we were smarter, we'd probably be scared, too."

"The tests, what can they prove?" asked Bobbi.

"That there are high concentrations of lead, arsenic, uranium, you name it, any nasty thing, it's there," answered Chris.

"Yeah, nice land to build a house on in a few years. You'd glow after the first week."

"Now what?"

"Frankly, I don't know," sighed Arnie. "This one is so big we can't afford to rush. And you know me well enough to know I don't run scared."

"Yeah," agreed Chris. "If any of the major players catch on to what we're into, before we've got enough evidence to blow this thing open—"

"And protect ourselves," interjected Arnie.

"That, too — they could hit us from any side."

"Like?" asked Bobbi.

"People disappear for a lot less," replied Arnie. "There's enough scum around that a fifty dollar bill will buy a knife in your heart, or your car wired with a few sticks of dynamite. You two could have a break-in some night and get beaten to death, likewise me. The police consider robbery the motive, case closed. Anything's possible." He stopped and took a long drink of his bloody mary and began to gasp.

"Next time, easy on the hot sauce, okay?"

Bobbi and Chris howled with laughter and Arnie added his throaty bellowing. They were scared and a good laugh was what they needed most.

"Not that I particularly want to throw a wet blanket on this fun party, kids," said Arnie as he wiped his eyes.

"Go on, party poop," whooped Bobbi.

"We've got a big unknown in our midst — actually more in yours since you guys mingle with the bluebloods."

"Shit! I forgot!" exclaimed Chris.

"What?" asked Bobbi, her smile fading.

"From all indications this whole thing is being masterminded by one of Tampa's own. And it's probable you guys brush elbows with mister big and regard him as just another rich bastard who can do no wrong. He might even be a personal friend. Just a word of caution, this guy has no regrets about killing. Anybody."

"Any ideas? Guesses?" asked Bobbi frowning.

"Garrett couldn't help us," responded Chris. "He was scared. The way a chicken knows a fox is hiding close by but the chicken doesn't know if it's wearing chicken feathers and is in the coop with him."

"Good analogy," said Arnie. "But remember this fox has the money, brains and power to stay way in the background and put so many layers of flunkies out in front it would take Charlie Chan to sort through the maze."

"Gee, thanks, Arnie. You're a real pal," quipped Bobbi.

"Huh?"

"Just when I was thinking all my little rich connections are plastic people whose greatest concern was the theme of their next party, you tell me one of them is actually made of plastique and could blow us apart."

"Yep."

Life was getting complicated — and dangerous.

LOVE AND DEATH

"Ummmm, that was wonderful," Bobbi whispered as Chris kissed her on the forehead and then rolled over to his side of the large bed. Their lovemaking was intense and deeply satisfying for them both. "Thank you," she said softly.

"Don't you know you should never thank a man for making love with him?" laughed Chris.

Bobbi turned on her stomach and propped herself up on her elbows. "Oh? And why is that?"

"Just because."

"One of your rules?"

"Maybe," he pulled her close and kissed her swollen lips. Their bodies pressed together and he could feel himself responding to the heat of her, the musky smell of her body.

"Oh, lady," he whispered huskily. "The things you do to me."

Bobbi rolled from his grasp and began inching down the bed, planting kisses along his body as she went.

"What things?" she giggled then sucked on his nipple.

"Those things," he gasped.

She continued trailing kisses down his chest and then flicked her tongue in the concave of his navel. He groaned and she slid down and took him in her mouth.

Theirs was lovemaking finely tuned to each other's body, born of a deep and trusting love. They were totally committed to each other.

"Wake up, lady." Chris placed a breakfast tray gently over Bobbi's prone form.

"Ummmmm, is that dessert?" Bobbi asked as she opened one eye.

"You could say that. You need something to keep your strength up — no, maybe I need something to keep my strength up. You wear me out, lady!"

Bobbi pushed herself up and opened her mouth to speak. Chris popped a melon slice into her mouth and bent down to kiss her as she chewed on the cool fruit.

"Interesting party last night, don't you agree?" asked Bobbi when Chris emerged from the shower.

"Marcella really knows how to bring all the plastic people together," said Bobbi.

"Don't forget, we were there."

"Sure, but we had a reason."

"You're saying the others didn't?" asked Chris as he ran a comb through his unruly wet hair.

"Their reason was they wanted to mingle with others of their kind."

"Sounds like a gathering at the zoo," laughed Chris.

"That's what most of those social functions remind me of. Animals strutting and puffing, putting on a show."

"Picky, picky, my dear," responded Chris in a falsetto voice.

"Oh, you know what I mean!"

"Yeah, afraid I do. Everyone's so damned concerned about the welfare of animals and yet did you catch all the fur coats?"

"Made me squirm."

Karen's phone call cut short their critique of Marcella's party. "Your friend Arnie," Karen said softly. "They just found his body."

DANGEROUS DECISIONS

"You did what?" Marcella demanded.

Herbert looked at her. "When I took over at Grand Enterprises after that Turlington woman's death, there were changes, immediate changes that were necessary. I've been taking care of them."

"Without discussing them with me first?" she yelled.

"Yes. I didn't think it necessary to bother you."

"Bother me? It's my company and you don't think it's necessary to bother me?" She spat out the words.

"I don't know why you're so upset, my dear," Herbert replied. Her outburst surprised him; it wasn't like Marcella to show such rage.

"You chauvinistic little twerp! Maybe you felt it was beyond my female capability to understand and make good business decisions?!"

"I didn't think that, although you have had a lot on your mind lately with Bobbi's accident—"

"And that gives you the right to run my business?!"

It had been a stupid mistake for Herbert to make. A mistake Marcella didn't plan on him living to regret. She cursed herself for getting so wrapped up in trying to protect herself from Bobbi's prying eyes that she hadn't stayed abreast of Herbert's activities. She had severely underestimated him. She'd deal with him once she had Bobbi completely under control.

When Bobbi came to her with information about the toxic dumping, she tried to convince Bobbi she was mistaken. Bobbi had persisted.

Hiring goons to dispose of Arnie was easy enough. He was lured to a midnight meeting by supposed informants, overpowered, filled full of his regular brand of scotch, knocked out and held under water. The police report called it an accidental drowning due to alcohol intoxication and closed their files despite Bobbi's and Chris' accusations of foul play.

But Bobbi wouldn't let up, insisting there was intrigue that spread its tentacles all the way to Washington. She had papers, charts, maps, chemical analyses done by out-of-state firms. She was more tenacious than ever.

Marcella finally agreed to help. She was trying to buy time, placate Bobbi, and keep her from going to someone else with her reams of papers, her accusations.

When Bobbi came to her naming the Achilles Chemical Company as the prime suspect dumping toxic waste into the borrow pit, Marcella knew she had to act. Achilles was her company, its ownership buried in a maze of false corporations and holding companies.

Chris died instantly when the tanker truck slammed into the Porsche. The driver of the tanker claimed he didn't see the Porsche stopped alongside the interstate, its lights out.

An inspection of the car indicated a complete electrical failure caused the Porsche to suddenly lose power. The tanker was in the wrong place at the wrong time. The newspapers called it an unfortunate accident.

Bobbi survived the accident. Her injuries were massive and her doctors held little hope for her ever seeing or walking again.

Marcella felt confident Bobbi's quest was over. The days she spent by her side in the hospital convinced her Bobbi was no longer a crusader. This Bobbi she no longer feared.

COINCIDENCE

"It's almost like we're all jinxed," said Candy.

"You don't really believe that?" asked Marcella.

They were again at the Garden Room for lunch, but there were only three at the table. Marcella. Candy. Karen. Three empty places were also set.

"It's spooky," continued Candy. "I'm the only one here who hasn't been hurt or had someone in my family die this year."

"Coincidental," said Marcella as she took a sip of vichyssoise.

"Maybe," replied Karen.

"Meaning?" Marcella asked nonchalantly. She hoped she wouldn't be forced to deal with Karen, too.

"Well, odds of so few people having so many fatal or near fatal occurrences within such a short span of time, I'd say they'd be quite phenomenal."

"Just what I meant," seconded Candy.

"Unfortunate, yes. Coincidence, yes. Something suspicious, no. Let's not let our grief cloud our thinking, shall we? Which reminds me, I saw Bobbi this morning. She's coming along fabulously. Such strength of mind that poor girl has."

"Now that's where I'm talking about coincidence," said Karen.

"Oh?"

"Yes. Bobbi and Chris were just about ready to blow the lid off some high level corruption when the accident happened."

"What on earth are you talking about?" asked Marcella.

"She told me she had irrefutable proof to tie in a local company with some illegal dumping. And she believed that reporter friend of theirs was murdered to scare them off."

"You have to be kidding," Marcella could feel a knot developing in her stomach.

"Real spy stuff?" asked Candy.

"I'm afraid it isn't as exciting as James Bond would have made it, but intrigue none the less," Karen replied.

"Sounds more like hallucinations to me," said Marcella.

"If you thought it was so ridiculous, why were you helping her?" asked Karen.

Marcella was dumbfounded.

"Bobbi and Chris had just left my house when the accident happened, remember?" Karen said. "The reason they stopped by was to give me the latest update on their investigation. The name of the chemical company, Antilles, I believe."

"Achilles—" Marcella corrected her and then stopped.

"Yes," Karen replied as she looked directly at Marcella.

Marcella carefully folded her napkin and placed it neatly by her plate.

"Why don't we have dinner tonight, about eight?" Marcella asked Karen. She needed time to think, to plan. And she needed to talk to Karen without witnesses.

Into The Spider's Web

"You're responsible for what happened to Bobbi, aren't you?"

Marcella looked at Karen. They were seated in Marcella's study. The downtown Tampa skyline, ablaze with lights, was visible through the watermarked silk covering the enormous bay windows.

"You *are* responsible, aren't you?" Karen repeated.

"That is an outrageous thing to ask, how could you possibly think that I—"

"Spare me. Achilles is your company—"

"You have no proof."

"It will be easy enough to trace."

"And what will that prove; assuming you do find it's mine?"

"It will prove that Bobbi made a terrible mistake in thinking you were her friend."

"And?"

"Perhaps it isn't just coincidental that so many in our group have suffered disastrous consequences in the past few months."

"What in hell are you insinuating?!"

"I'm just saying perhaps not everything has happened without a little assistance," Karen spoke softly and watched as Marcella's demeanor changed. She saw the tightening at the corners of her eyes, a pinching of her lips. A chill shot through her as she realized Marcella might have had something to do with the accident that killed Chris and gravely injured Bobbi.

"Karen," said Marcella. "We're all looking around corners lately! My God, look at what each of us has been through! First, Charles unexpected death. Then Sandra's drug overdose. And my poor Ed. I hesitate to mention Cissy. Who wouldn't get a bit paranoid?"

The tension in Marcella's face was replaced by a teary-eyed smile. Karen mentally reprimanded herself for having doubted her friend.

"And, yes, I'll admit Achilles is my company. Sometimes I forget just how many little corporations my father snapped up when he heard they were on the brink of financial ruin. You know he was a great businessman that way. And Ed, he used to have the same knack. Poor Ed. He could pick a good business but he didn't recognize a good woman when he had one."

Marcella reached for the baccarat decanter and poured herself another splash of brandy. She offered some brandy to Karen but Karen waved it away.

A matching decanter held Karen's favorite cognac, Courvoisier. Marcella had replenished the crystal decanter's contents earlier in the day. Anticipating that Karen would limit herself to only one refill, Marcella added what she calculated to be a lethal dose of barbiturates.

"Honestly, though, Karen," Marcella lowered her voice to a whisper. "I am quite concerned."

"How so?"

"It's difficult for me to say this, but I'm worried, and I might add, more than a bit scared."

She removed the crystal stopper from the decanter of cognac and refilled Karen's glass.

"It's Herbert," she said.

"Herbert?" Karen asked incredulously.

"You know that I was close to his first wife? Of course that was long before you and I met. You would have liked her."

"You've talked about her, yes."

"Well, I thought it was her illness, you know, the cancer, making her say foolish things. Many people do start imagining things when they're undergoing such tremendous stresses in their lives."

"Yes."

"Toward the end, she told me that Herbert was a big mafia boss, that he was responsible for killings, things like that."

"Herbert?!" Karen exclaimed in disbelief.

"Yes. I've known Herbert for what seems almost all my life, and there was just no way I could believe that sweet man was involved in anything the least bit shady. Much less see him as a godfather, for Pete's sake," Marcella paused.

"And something changed your mind?"

"Circumstances. Nothing really substantial, I'm afraid. It's just there are so many circumstances, coincidences. Remember when Candy and you were talking at the restaurant at lunch how unusual, and coincidental, it is for all of us to have experienced tragedy in such a short time?"

"Yes."

"While I listened to you, pieces started fitting together. Now I'm even more scared."

"Go on."

"First, when Ed died, Herbert took over control of Grand Enterprises, behind the scene. He's always been my advisor of sorts. He's a very shrewd businessman. He said he found some mismanagement of funds and he thought Cissy was responsible. He was very angry when he told me. I'd never seen him so angry. He said he'd take care of it and a week later Cissy was dead."

Karen looked stunned.

"You think Herbert had something to do—"

"I don't know, but he didn't seem surprised about her death. As a matter of fact—" Marcella stopped and her eyes widened as though she were seeing something for the first time.

"What?"

"He said," Marcella replied, drawing out the words. "That nobody steals from him, not even an oversexed tramp. Those were his words. I'd never heard him talk like that before. He seemed like a completely different person. I should never have told him about Bobbi, it's all my fault."

"What are you talking about? What about Bobbi?"

"Bobbi would come over, we'd talk. She's such a sweet young thing, and so honest. Well, Herbert took an avid interest in what Bobbi and Chris and that newspaper friend of theirs were doing. I mean, thinking back, he took an obsessive interest, wanting to know everything she'd told me after each of her visits. And I, like a blind fool, told him everything."

"You're saying—"

"Herbert controls Achilles, not me. A couple times I asked him about their activities and he changed the subject. Looking back, I realize how strange his actions were. And then that reporter friend of theirs drowns and they have that horrible accident."

"And now you're not sure it was an accident?"

"I don't know what to think," Marcella said softly. It was going well she thought. A brilliant stroke to point the finger at Herbert, make it appear she herself might have something to fear. It actually didn't matter what she said, she was stalling for time until the barbiturates in Karen's cognac took effect. Karen would be dead within a matter of hours and she'd have only two loose ends left to tie up. Bobbi and Herbert.

"Why are you telling me this?" asked Karen.

"Who else can I tell? You know how close Herbert is with the power brokers in this town. I don't know who to trust," she stopped. "Frankly, I'm scared for my own life now."

Karen drained her glass.

"I can understand what you're going through, but if he is a murderer, he's got to be stopped.

Marcella was delighted. Her ploy has working, just as it should have worked with Bobbi.

Karen started to rise from the velvet upholstered loveseat. She hesitated and sat back down.

"I don't think I should have had so much to drink," she said as she drew a breath and stood up.

"You know you're welcome to stay in our guest room tonight," offered Marcella solicitously.

"No, I have a short drive and I feel fine, really," answered Karen. "I think I've been sitting too long."

"You'll be careful?" asked Marcella as she walked Karen to the door.

"Of course, and you watch yourself. If you're correct, you are in the gravest danger."

Marcella smiled as she closed and locked the ornately carved door. Goodbye, old friend, she whispered as she leaned against the door.

ALIVE BY DEFAULT

Instead of going directly home after leaving Marcella's, Karen stopped to talk with John Cunningham, the doctor who was overseeing Bobbi's progress. John lived in a condo three floors down from Marcella and Herbert.

John turned out to be a friend to whom Karen could turn whenever she needed a confidant.

It was at John's home that Karen's convulsions began. His fast action saved her life. Had she gone straight home, she would have died in a car crash or in her sleep as Marcella had planned.

The weeks that followed were time-consuming and chaotic for Marcella. She continued her daily trips to check on Bobbi's progress. And then Bobbi was transferred to Sea Castle convalescent center, a particularly pricey establishment where patients resided in tastefully appointed suites and medical attendants wore pastels instead of stark white. The transfer had been Marcella's idea. She wanted Bobbi away from where machines kept Karen alive and away from John Cunningham's close scrutiny.

Since the accident Bobbi appeared to have lost almost all will to live even though her physical progress was excellent. The blindness had been temporary and she needed only the assistance of a cane to walk. However, Marcella was determined to make certain she never regained her confidence, or her memory of the days prior to the accident.

Marcella marveled at how tenaciously Bobbi fought to survive at the beginning of her hospitalization, before she learned Chris died at the accident scene.

Doctor Cunningham wanted Bobbi to be kept sedated and unaware of the details of the accident, but Marcella distracted the young afternoon nursing aide, kept her from administering the necessary sedatives. Later, when Bobbi was in a fitful semi-awakened state, Marcella told her in graphic detail about the accident, Chris' massive injuries. She embroidered the truth with visions of Chris pinned in the burning car, screaming as his very life was sucked from him. And, when Marcella had finished, Bobbi had lapsed into a traumatized emotional state of mind.

Marcella continued to spend long hours at Bobbi's bedside recounting in low monotones Chris' last terrible moments until Bobbi would awake screaming in the night.

Karen, too, had spent time at Bobbi's bedside. She was unable to understand Bobbi's complete mental collapse. She assumed Bobbi was stronger, particularly after the many discussions they'd had in previous weeks. To Karen it was peculiar that Bobbi seemed to sink further into mental darkness after Marcella's visits. She mentioned her concerns to John Cunningham.

And then she confronted Marcella and Karen herself now was a victim, having barely survived the encounter. For Marcella, Karen's condition was no threat. She was vegetative and it would be merely a matter of time before Doctor Cunningham would approach her about consent papers to disconnect the machines that were keeping her alive.

Marcella, of course, told Bobbi about Karen's apparent suicide attempt — for that was how Marcella portrayed Karen's barbiturate collapse to all who would listen. Karen was upset over Bobbi's injuries, Chris' death. She was still mourning her husband. And, according to Marcella, Karen had talked in irrational terms about Sandra's and Cissy's deaths. Marcella stretched the truth to fit the occasion and before long their circle of friends was convinced Karen had tried to take her own life.

Bobbi's reaction to Karen's condition surprised Marcella. For the first time in weeks, Bobbi began talking to Marcella. Her thoughts were rambling patches and pieces but yet someone who was looking for such patches and pieces, such as John Cunningham, who was showing an extraordinary interest in both Bobbi and Karen, might be able to put them together. And they might lead to Marcella.

It wouldn't do, this new emotional strength Bobbi was developing, and Marcella knew just exactly how to get her back to the passive creature she had been. She began again with even more impassioned stories of Chris and the accident. Chris so badly mangled the police required dental records to make a positive identification, so charred, so mutilated that the morticians insisted cremation was mandatory. Bobbi's relapse was swift.

Marcella chose Sea Castle convalescent center for Bobbi, since she knew Sea Castle's security was lax. She needed Bobbi somewhere that she could be permanently silenced should, or more accurately when, it became necessary. She was certain it was only a matter of time before Bobbi again became lucid, and she didn't expect to spend the rest of her life playing mind games, forcing Bobbi back into safe territory.

Doctor Cunningham had not been easy to convince that Bobbi would be better off at Sea Castle. However,

Marcella enlisted the aid of several of their friends who talked to him and, using arguments supplied by Marcella, suggested that Bobbi might respond to a change of scenery.

Bobbi's condition was termed recuperative so she no longer had need of the hospital's medical supervision and services. A pleasant environment such as that at Sea Castle might bring her around. John Cunningham oversaw her transfer despite gnawing doubts. Medically, he had no reason to keep her in the hospital.

MIND GAMES

Karen listened for the comforting hiss of air rushing into the chamber. Air molecules smashed together as the atmospheric pressure changed.

She cleared her ears by swallowing hard and wished there was some other way to stop the sharp stabbing pains that kept assaulting her eardrums each time she entered the chamber.

She took deep measured breaths of pure oxygen and waited for the "ting" of the timer that signaled the air exchange within the chamber.

Karen turned her attention back to the gauges. She felt a certain comfort seeing Bonnie's placid face peering down at her. It added a personal touch to an impersonal, albeit necessary, daily function. Too bad Bonnie was getting so old.

Karen heard the sharp "ting" and looked at the countdown clock. Twenty minutes. She looked at the other gauges. If she were under the sea, she'd be at 4500 feet.

She closed her eyes and drifted into the dreamless sleep state the chamber sometimes produced.

Oxygen hissed into the chamber. She opened her eyes, looked at the gauges. Everything was functioning efficiently.

She slipped deeper toward the fragile netherworld of death.

"Doctor," whispered Bonnie to the stolid figure standing next to her. "Doctor, there's been no change from earlier brain scans."

The monitors reflected erratic spiking lines. There was activity but it no longer was that of a normal brain. Her eyes roamed the room but there was no sign of recognition. And Karen's body refused to function on its own. The damage from the drug overdose had been appalling, paralyzing virtually all physical function and, from all signs, causing massive brain tissue destruction.

"I can see that, nurse," he replied sharply.

"All I meant—"

"The decision will be made in due time," he muttered as he walked quickly from the room. He was angry. The patient was a friend, a very special friend, and he didn't relish the task before him. Even more insidious was the knowledge that the vegetative woman on life support was the only link, the one witness whose testimony could unveil a murderer. And now she was dangerously close to becoming another victim.

He was striding angrily to the nurses' station when Marcella grabbed his arm.

"John?" she asked. "How is she? I've been sitting here for hours."

"She remains on life support."

"Will she recover? John, she must recover!" Marcella gave a dramatic performance.

"I frankly—"

"John?"

"She's nearly brain dead, dammit!" he shouted.

Aides turned to stare.

"Oh, god!" Marcella put her hands to her face.

"I'll need your approval to turn the machines off," he said angrily.

"Mine?" Marcella asked quietly.

"She did give you her power-of-attorney, didn't she? And there is a living will!" He didn't attempt to contain his anger.

"Yes."

"Then your signature will be necessary before we disconnect the machines — should we need to." He turned and stalked away. He knew Marcella was responsible for Karen's condition, and he had every reason to suspect Bobbi was another of her victims. But knowing and proving were two different matters.

Marcella put a tissue to her mouth to cover her smile. Foolish, foolish Karen.

DOCTOR IN THE HOUSE

For John Cunningham, Bobbi's progress was an enigma but his concern for Karen consumed the majority of his waking hours. His was more than professional interest as he had fallen deeply in love with her. She was the first woman to whom he had been so drawn, so mentally attuned, for whom he had felt such a strong physical attraction since his wife died five years before. Though she had no idea the depth of his caring for her, he was on the verge of bringing his feelings out in the open when she collapsed in his apartment.

Karen had also been drawn to John. She found him easy to confide in, a man who possessed extraordinary common sense, who wasn't intimidated by money or power. She told him as much as she could about Bobbi's investigations, Bobbi's suspicions that Arnie's death hadn't been an accident, and that she and Chris were certain they had been followed on numerous occasions since Arnie's death.

On their last night together, Karen was in the middle of recounting her earlier conversation with Marcella when her convulsions began. John had never really liked Marcella, though he had no specific reason that he could identify. Now he considered her solicitous attitude cloying.

Although Karen was, for all reasonable medical purposes, brain dead and vegetative, John did not plan on giving Marcella the chance to have Karen's life support turned off until he exhausted every medical option available. He fully expected Marcella to remain quiet and cooperative as he felt she had no reason to do otherwise.

Three weeks after Bobbi's transfer to Sea Castle she was visited by her stepsister and her husband. It was Karen had told John Cunningham, during one of their earlier conversations, of Bobbi's parents' tragic death and Bobbi's adoption by her elderly aunt and uncle. It was the memory of this conversation that inspired John to seek out Bobbi's family and tell them of her present situation.

Joanne and Bill Snyder were lovely, warm people who immediately made arrangements to move Bobbi to their spacious Cape Cod estate after the necessary releases had been signed and a copy of Bobbi's medical file had been delivered to the Snyder's personal physician. A registered nurse was employed to oversee Bobbi's daily needs.

Marcella was frantic. Bobbi couldn't be moved, it just wasn't possible. She had to stay in Florida. She had to stay in Sea Castle. She had to die.

Joanne Snyder, a no-nonsense type of woman in her early fifties met with Marcella. She tried to calm the woman who had taken such a strong interest in her stepsister. Yes, she did know that Bobbi had suffered numerous traumas. Yes, she did understand that Bobbi was quite mentally fragile. She also knew that Bobbi could be best helped if she was surrounded by her own family. Joanne intended to provide a warm, soothing atmosphere in which Bobbi could recuperate at her own pace. Marcella was free to visit whenever she wished.

It was the last thing Marcella could have anticipated, this uncovering of Bobbi's family and their quick removal of Bobbi from Sea Castle. She also had not anticipated Doctor Cunningham's rapid processing of the papers, his quick approval of Bobbi's release into another physician's custody. Almost as though he knew. But knew what? Thoughts of exposure kept racing through Marcella's brain.

But there was more to worry about. She still had to deal with Herbert's manipulations of Grand Enterprises. And she had to make certain that Karen died, the quicker the better.

LOSING CONTROL

Marcella had meant to take swift action against Herbert after he told her he'd been making business decisions without her knowledge. She'd displayed uncustomary anger toward Herbert which surprised him and she'd had every intention of killing him the same way she'd killed Ed. But then, within hours of their confrontation, Karen proved to be a more serious threat and Marcella was forced to turn her attention toward the more immediate danger that Karen posed.

With Karen for all purposes dead and Bobbi a thousand miles away, Marcella turned her attention again to Herbert.

"More coffee, darling?" Marcella asked and nodded to Alice to refill Herbert's cup.

"Thank you, my dear," said Herbert as he raised the steaming cup to his lips.

It had been weeks since they'd sat down at the same table for breakfast. More precisely, not since the morning Marcella vented her anger over Herbert's manipulations of Grand Enterprises.

"And, my dear, what have you heard of Bobbi's progress?"

"That woman won't let me speak with her," Marcella said through pursed lips.

Herbert couldn't understand why Marcella was so upset about Bobbi's release into her stepsister's care. He hadn't known Marcella to be excessively fond of Bobbi prior to her accident, and it seemed a bit odd that she now took Bobbi's progress so personally. He attributed her attitude to misplaced maternal instinct, likening Bobbi to the daughter she never had.

"Joanne?" asked Herbert.

"No, that nurse of hers."

"Then, my dear, if it will make you feel better, why don't you fly up and see for yourself that she's in good hands. And have a talk with the nurse."

"I was planning on doing that," replied Marcella.

"Good. And now, as much as I hate to discuss such things with you, particularly considering all that you've had on your mind—"

"What is it?" Marcella snapped.

"We've had an offer to sell the shipyard. I turned it down, of course."

Marcella looked at him sharply. And then she smiled. "Herbert, you always know the right thing to do. I have complete confidence in you."

He was stunned as he expected another outburst. He looked closely at her. Her hair was uncombed, she wore no makeup, and her clothes hung on her gaunt frame. This wasn't the Marcella he knew.

Marcella got up from the table and walked slowly to her bedroom. Once she had closed and locked the door she collapsed on the massive bed. She felt as though her mind was exploding. As much as she tried to hold herself together things kept crowding her, making it impossible for her to keep control.

She was used to being in control. Since she'd learned as a small child that she could make her grandmother and her father do as she wished — her grandmother much more so than her father — she had been able to manipulate those around her.

But, where she had been able to steer her little group, Bobbi, Karen, Candy, Sandra and that obnoxious Cissy, in directions she chose, everything had now changed.

She put her hands to her temples and pressed hard, trying to relieve the immense feeling of pressure that pushed against her skull. It was as though her brain was expanding fourfold and would either split open her skull or implode.

It had happened before, this feeling. Twice before. The first time was when she found out she was pregnant. It was during her second year of marriage to Ed. She hadn't told him of her pregnancy. She planned on telling him after a romantic candlelight dinner, but that same day she found out he was having an affair with his secretary.

She drove to Lakeland, parked her car, and took a taxi to an abortionist working out of a sleazy office in Bartow. It had been quick, she was only a couple months along, but the scraping and probing had been enough to make her sterile. She didn't find out about that until years later.

By the time she got home she realized what she had done and her mind went on vacation for almost two weeks. It was a breakdown, but not so severe that she couldn't function fairly normally for its duration. She had no memory of those several days other than the intermittent crying spells when she was alone. And she didn't remember exactly what she did to get over it, just that one day she was better. She believed that her sterility was equitable punishment for Ed's infidelity, since he was so anxious to become a father.

The next time the feeling came over her and the telltale signals began, she was going through some of her father's private correspondence when she came across the pictures. Why hadn't he destroyed them?

And the letters. She could feel her mind expanding as she stuffed the vile pictures and crudely worded correspondence into a trash can and threw in a lighted match.

After her father's death she didn't have to pretend to function normally, everyone allowed her time to grieve. Her mental collapse fit perfectly into a normal mourning pattern. That she would not speak about him and ran from the room if his name was mentioned, that too was considered part of her deep grieving. She allowed them to believe as they wished.

And now it was happening again. She'd covered her tracks so carefully with Sandra's death. It had been imperative to get rid of the insufferable creature so that when she murdered Ed, Herbert would be easily accessible. While she'd wished Cissy ill, and she fully intended to eliminate her in due time, she had been as surprised as everyone else when Cissy died.

Hiring thugs to take care of Arnie had been somewhat precarious since she'd never involved anyone else in her dealings. But she paid the killers a substantial amount of money for the job, and they did it well without telltale signs that would stir up an investigation, then they quietly left town.

She again had to involve others to kill Bobbi and Chris. While they had done what they called "an adequate job for the money," it had not been good enough since Bobbi was still alive and a threat.

She couldn't let her mind collapse. It just wasn't possible. She had to stay in complete control until they were all safely tucked away in their coffins.

She felt like screaming. It would feel good to let out a bloodcurdling scream. To force the feelings up from deep within her gut, push them out into the light where she could confront them, squash them. While they were so knotted within her she felt powerless.

Goddamn it, snap out of it!

"Oh, fine, now I'm talking to myself."

Yeah, well better you talk to yourself than to others right now, considering the state you're in. You're a real mess.

"Shut up!"

What's the matter? Can't stand the truth? Hey, babes, it was your idea to wipe out all the little people as you call them.

"They are!"

We both know that, babes. It's just that you can't seem to handle the heat when it gets a little rough.

"A little rough? You go down with me, you know."

That's why I'm not going to let you handle this on your own.

"Meaning?"

I've always been here. Now you need my help.

"You? How?"

You need someone you can trust, someone in your corner. Someone you can bounce ideas around with. That's me. If you can't trust yourself, who can you trust?

Marcella looked at her reflection in the mirror. "That's right, if I can't trust myself, who can I trust?"

Now you got it, babes. It's you and me. So let's start tackling all those persistent little annoyances systematically, shall we?

"Mmmmmmm."

First priority is to establish contact with Bobbi. She's been out from under your control for much too long. She could emerge from the twilight zone any time.

"That bitch nurse won't let me talk to her!"

That's why you're going to do just as you told Herbert. You're going to pay a visit to Bobbi. Now. And when you do, you'll twist that keeper of hers around your little finger like you so ably do. Then you'll come back here and control her from here.

"How, for chrissakes?!"

Come on, I've heard you on the phone.

"Of course! You're right!"

See? Not so difficult when you've got someone to help you. But you've got to do something about the way you look. Jesus! You can't let yourself go like you have.

"Oh!"

Now here's what you do. Call Zarita's and tell her she must take you in immediately. Get the works. Facial, mas-

sage, body wrap, waxing, manicure, perm. After you have an appointment with Zarita, call and get an evening flight to Cape Cod. Forget about calling the Snyder's. Just show up. They've already said it was okay, and if they seem the least bit annoyed tell them you kept getting a busy signal and you thought perhaps the phone lines were down. You'll think of something.

"You're right, I will. I always do."

STRATEGIC PLANNING

Marcella's taxi dropped her off at the Snyder's home a few minutes after midnight. Joanne and Bill were gracious hosts, accepted her explanation of unsuccessful attempts to reach them by phone, and gave her the room next to Bobbi's. Bobbi was sleeping. There would be plenty of time in the morning to say hello.

Yes, Bobbi was doing wonderfully. She was responding well to physical therapy, now able to take long walks through the woods. She still had her withdrawn periods but they had every confidence that soon there'd be a major breakthrough.

See? Aren't you glad you listened to me?

"Yes."

We'll take a little walk through the woods with Bobbi tomorrow. Alone. We'll put a stop to her grand progress. All you have to do is make certain that bitch nurse doesn't tag along.

"Okay."

"Bobbi, you look absolutely fantastic!"

Bobbi turned and smiled a weak smile. "So-do-you-Mar-cella."

Despite herself Marcella felt pity for the girl. She had a difficult time believing this was the same Bobbi, the vivacious mountain climbing, skydiving, devil-may-care Bobbi she used to envy. Envy! She'd never thought in those terms about Bobbi before.

Maybe not consciously, babes, but I've known all along.

"I've missed you, Bobbi. I've called to talk to you, but your nurse won't let me through."

"She-is-nice-lady."

"I know that. It's just, you know how concerned I am, how much I care about you!" She wrapped an arm around Bobbi's waist and drew her close. Bobbi stiffened her body and Marcella released her hold.

The woods were cool. Light streamed in ribbons through the treetops. A carpet of discarded leaves covered the ground and crunched under their footsteps.

Bobbi's nurse wanted to accompany them on their walk but Marcella smiled sweetly, patted her on the hand, and assured her she was perfectly capable of seeing that Bobbi got back safely.

"You're looking so very much better than when you were in that horrid hospital."

"Yes-very-much-better."

"Do you remember the hospital?"

Bobbi shook her head.

"What about that nice place you went afterwards?"

Bobbi again shook her head.

"What do you remember?" Marcella asked softly as though she were talking to a child.

"Re-mem-ber?"

"Yes. You must remember something. Do you know who I am?"

"Mar-cel-la."

"Yes, but your nurse told you that just a little while ago."

"Mar-cel-la."

"Do you remember Sandra?"

"San-dra?"

"Do you remember Candy?"

"Can-dee?"

"Do you remember Karen?"

Bobbi stopped walking. "Karen?! Karen!? Is-Kar-ren-here?"

Marcella stopped and stared at Bobbi.

"I-want-to-see-Kar-ren!" She sounded like a petulant child.

See, she does remember. You're a fool if you let her get away from you this time.

"What can I do?"

First, stop acting like a child!

"I'm not!"

Yes you are. Do you want my help or not?

"Of course I do."

That's better. Take a deep breath and let's work this thing through, just like we've done before.

"It would make Chris very unhappy if you talked to Karen." Bobbi's eyes widened. "Karen murdered Chris. He told me."

"Chris-told-" Bobbi slurred the words.

"Chris wants you with him. He loves you. He wants to protect you from Karen."

Bobbi stared at Marcella then let out a loud wail, turned and ran through the woods.

Searchers found Bobbi several hours later, lying in a clump of wildflowers. She refused to walk or talk and had to be carried back to her room.

Marcella flew home the following day. She waited one more day before calling the Snyder's home. Bobbi's nurse answered the phone.

"Hello, Mrs. Simpson, this is Marcella."

Marcella smirked at her reflection in her mirror as she listened to the nurse's voice.

"Oh, yes, I had an excellent flight home. But I've been so worried about Bobbi. How is she doing?" Marcella blinked and then smiled as she listened.

"Oh, that's too bad. Complete collapse? But she seemed so happy and peaceful when I was there before— I had no idea. Perhaps if you could let me talk to her for a couple minutes?"

Marcella knew this was the risky part. The nurse had no good cause not to hand the telephone over to Bobbi, but then again, she had acted so protectively during Marcella's previous phone calls. "I won't talk to her long. I just want to say hello, that's all."

She could hear Mrs. Simpson talking to Bobbi, telling her she had a friend who wanted to say hello on the telephone. There were sounds of shuffling feet and a clattering as the receiver was picked up, dropped and retrieved. Marcella heard Mrs. Simpson tell Bobbi that she would be back in a couple minutes.

"'Low?" It was a guttural sound.

"Bobbi, my love, don't say a word, just listen." Marcella spoke in a deep hoarse whisper. "Karen murdered me. She made that truck hit your car and she paid them to let me burn. Oh, it hurt so much. I felt it all as my skin melted and fell away from my bones. But I'm in a safe place now and I want you to join me. Please, you will join me now, won't you, my love? I've been so lonely—"

A piercing scream came through the telephone and Marcella smiled as she heard the receiver crash to the floor.

There were sounds of running feet and then Mrs. Simpson picked up the phone.

"My god, what happened?" Marcella asked. She smiled as she listened to the nurse. "She's what? But I was telling her how much we all missed her and about Candy's wedding. Surely that couldn't have upset her?" She simpered at the mirror and smoothed her vermillion red lipstick with her little finger.

"Of course I understand. Please, I'll call again tomorrow to see how she'd doing. Thank you so much for your kindness." Marcella hung up the telephone and patted her hair.

"Think that should do it?" asked Bobbi as she turned the tape recorder off.

John Cunningham looked at her and then nodded his head. "I've got to get back quickly. I've given instructions that no one is to be allowed near Karen but if Marcella believes you're safely out of her hair for a while she may take another try at her before we can get our case to the authorities."

"I never would have believed it if you would have told me two months ago that Marcella was a murderess," said Bobbi.

"Karen was suspicious—"

"I know, but I stupidly didn't listen to her."

"Don't blame yourself. Karen may die because she didn't take her own suspicions seriously enough. Incidentally, you've been magnificent these last few weeks. Without your help, we wouldn't have known for certain that Marcella was responsible for what happened to Chris, Karen and you."

"Shall we say we make a good couple of detectives, doctor?"

"And you're one mighty fine actress."

"Maybe murder brings out the best in me. And it certained helped having a skilled doctor who could keet me alive to develop my theatrical skills."

"She'll call again."

"Oh, I'm counting on it." She tapped the tape recorder. "We'll keep the charade going until we have enough evidence that no grand jury in the country could fail to indict her. Besides, I need to play with her a bit so she'll stay away from Karen."

"Yes, that could help."

"Doctor, your honest opinion. From the heart, if that's what it takes. Will Karen ever recover?"

Dr. Cunningham hesitated and Bobbi could see the mistiness in his eyes. "Honestly? I don't know. I'm trying a few things now, and there are some very progressive medical professionals who are studying her case. Maybe, just an outside chance—"

Bobbi walked over and wrapped her arms around him and kissed his cheek. "You love her, don't you?"

He nodded.

"Did she know?"

"I waited too late—" he turned away.

"You'll get your chance to tell her," said Bobbi. "You're a good man. And she's one of the finest women I've ever known."

Less than five hours later, John Cunningham was again at Karen's bedside.

"Any change?" John asked the RN sitting next to Karen's hospital bed. He flipped through the pages of notations contained in the file he had taken from the nurses' station.

"None, doctor," replied the nurse. He leaned over, shined a light into Karen's eyes.

Between Heaven And Earth

Karen was standing in the rotunda of the immense building. Light poured in through huge skylights. She put a hand up to shade her eyes then turned to study the roster before she walked toward the bank of elevators. The elevator in front of her opened with a quiet "whoosh" and she stepped inside.

"What floor, please?" asked the computerized control system.

"Eight," answered Karen. She was looking for answers; perhaps the museum would hold them.

"Eighth floor, please watch your step, thank you."

She had been avoiding the museum. It housed too many painful memories from the past. But now she had to see if her future was somehow being controlled by her past.

She stood at the entrance to the museum and placed her encoded identification card into the slot. There was a buzzing and the doors opened. She stepped inside. She was alone. The doors closed softly behind her.

There were rows upon rows of displays. The material had been gathered from such impeccable sources as the Smithsonian Institute, the Louvre, and the Vatican. Numerous art museums' treasures were here as were countless artifacts that, during the twentieth century, had been considered too insignificant to safeguard for the future.

Karen wandered through the corridors viewing bits and pieces of the life she once lived.

"Doctor! The scan!"
"Turn the recorder on, nurse! And keep it running!"

Sharp voices disrupted her concentration and Karen turned to see where they had come from. When she saw no one, she walked toward another corridor, hesitated, then continued walking. Suddenly, a wave of loneliness swept over her, a wave so intense that she felt as though she might faint.

"Blood pressure is dropping!"

Karen reached out and grasped a handrail to steady herself.

"Doctor, her hand!" The RN watched as Karen's hand clenched tightly.

"I can see it nurse. Keep watching those monitors and tell me the second there's any change!"

Karen felt herself falling into blackness.

"We almost lost her," Dr. Cunningham told Bobbi by phone later that day. "I thought we were close to a breakthrough. The brain scan was less erratic. And, for the first time, she actually moved her fingers. No, it was more. She balled up her hand like she was holding something in it, or maybe holding onto something. And then everything went flat."

"And now?"

"She's stabilized, that's about it. Marcella was in the hospital at the time."

"How did she react?"

"I'd have to say her response to our almost losing Karen was about what I'd expect. She was having a difficult time concealing her disappointment that Karen didn't die."

"That witch!"

"Right now I'm more concerned with getting Karen back to where we had her today. Her room is under twenty-four hour guard so I don't think she's in any immediate danger. By the way, how are you doing?"

"I have another interesting phone conversation for you to listen to, doctor."

"More of the same?"

"More of the same. She's a very sick woman besides being so dangerous."

"I know. It's a shame we didn't find out earlier."

"No one would have believed us. They wouldn't now if it weren't for the tapes and even with them we have a tough case to build."

Nipped In The Bud

"Oh, my dear," Marcella said reproachingly. "We could have had such a beautiful wedding for you right here."

"Jimmy and I just wanted to keep it very simple," said Candy. A wide gold band circled her left ring finger.

"But it would have been such fun," said Marcella. "We could have had Henri cater a dinner, and hired a little dance band. And flowers! Every bride needs to be surrounded by beautiful flowers!"

"Marcella, please, it was sweet, really," said Candy. She and Jimmy were one of four couples married at the courthouse that day, and each couple smiled and held hands while the others were married by the court clerk. Then the eight newlyweds, unknown to each other prior to their meeting earlier at the courthouse, went to dinner together. Later, they drank toasts to themselves and each other in the quiet bar. And, much later, when the jukebox played "My Prayer," the four couples waltzed blissfully unaware of anyone else on the small dance floor.

"Are you listening to me?" demanded Marcella.

"Oh, I'm sorry, I was daydreaming."

"Well, now that you're married, and without even telling me — I'm very hurt, you know, see if you can't keep your mind on business," Marcella said sharply.

"Yes, ma'am," Candy bowed her head. She was looking forward to the day when she would be able to quit her job and stay home to take care of her children. She was surprised at how much she wanted to have children and Jimmy was just as enthusiastic to start a family.

While she was grateful to Marcella, she was uncomfortable with the changes she'd seen in her in the last several months. It was as though she was working for a stranger, a stranger with a volatile temper.

"Incidentally, order some more flowers for Karen's room."

Candy knew it would do no good to remind her again that flowers were not allowed in intensive care. She placed the order and gave instructions to the florist to deliver them to the nurses' station. At least they'd brighten up the hospital corridor.

"Did you order those flowers like I told you to?" Marcella asked an hour later.

"Yes, yellow roses, just as before," said Candy.

"You dumb creature! I've never told you to send yellow, never! Always red!" screamed Marcella.

"It's always been yellow, those were your instructions," said Candy quietly.

"Look, you cretin, just pack your things and get out! If you can't get a simple thing like ordering red roses right, heaven only knows what else you'll screw up!"

Candy picked up her purse, smoothed her dress and walked toward the door. "Goodbye, Marcella," she said.

Marcella picked up a crystal paperweight and threw it as the door closed.

One Last Toast

"Bobbi, this is Candy, and I don't know if you can even understand what I'm going to say, but I need to talk to someone and you're the only one I could think of. Oh, please, you don't even have to answer me, just stay on the line," Candy cried into the telephone.

Bobbi had the recorder turned on. She didn't believe Candy was malicious enough to harm her, but since Candy did work for Marcella, she was cautious. When the call came through, Joanne didn't tell Candy that Bobbi's condition had improved. It was part of the trap that had been set for Marcella.

"Bobbi?"

"Mmmmmmm."

"Oh, Bobbi, I wish things were like they used to be with all of us together, laughing, talking. I'd even be glad to listen to Cissy saying all those mean things. Oh, it's so terrible, and now Marcella."

"Mmmmmmm?"

"I know you don't understand what I'm saying, but she used to be so nice. I mean, she was always giving parties, and the wonderful times she and I used to have when we'd go on trips. She's not like that any more. I don't know what happened to her. I mean, it's not like she's upset about when you got hurt, she's angry. And she's even angrier when she talks about Karen. And poor Karen, lying in that hospital with wires and tubes attached to her body. It's awful, that's what it is. But Marcella just keeps demanding to know when she's going to die. I don't understand. Honest, I don't understand." She started sobbing.

"Can-dee?" Bobbi asked.

"Yes! Yes, Bobbi, it's Candy! Oh, it's good to hear you say my name! Listen to me blubbering like a child. Like I have a reason to cry, and you don't. You're so brave. And, Bobbi, I wish you could meet Jimmy. He's my husband. Can you believe it? Me, married? He's wonderful, just wonderful. But he wouldn't understand about Marcella, and about how it used to be with all of us."

"Can-dee, come visit?"

"I don't know," Candy said slowly. "Yes, yes, maybe I could. Yes, I will!"

Candy immediately called Marcella and asked that Marcella put her paycheck in the mail along with her unused vacation pay. Marcella was in good spirits and suggested that Candy stop by to pick up the check instead.

It was on the way to the airport that Candy's brain hemorrhaged; she was dead when Jimmy carried her into the hospital emergency room.

Up In Smoke

"She was on her way to see me. She was upset about Marcella, she needed to talk," said Bobbi.

"Her husband's completely shattered, I'm having a hard time talking to him to piece together the hours before she died. But one thing I've been able to learn, she was at Marcella's earlier in the day," said John Cunningham. "Now, I have another problem on my hands."

"Marcella?"

"Very perceptive. She's taken Candy's husband under her wing like a protective mother hen. I can't pull her away from him. Not only that, she's rushing him about the funeral and the poor kid's so distraught, he's not fighting her."

"What're you going to do?"

"Not too much I can do about the funeral preparations, but right now her body is not being released until a complete autopsy has been performed. And this one I'm taking a personal interest in."

"What do you expect to find?"

"I'm not certain, but you've said Candy didn't do drugs—"

"Not that I'm aware of," said Bobbi.

"So barbiturates and hard drugs shouldn't be a favor unlike the results of Sandra's autopsy?"

"Of course not! Everyone knew Sandra had a bad drug habit, at least everyone except Herbert."

"Cissy had a drug habit, too?"

"Well, no, but—" Bobbi hesitated.

"But, what? She was full of drugs."

"Well, she kept to herself more than the others," said Bobbi.

"So it's possible she was as much a druggie as Sandra?"

"I suppose. It just doesn't seem likely, though."

"I'll call you later. Right now, I've got to beef up the security around Karen and then talk to the medical examiner."

The autopsy turned up nothing suspicious, no drug abuse, nothing. The toxicologist's report would take about twenty-four hours, and tissue samples were taken for further tests, but it appeared Candy's death was due to natural causes. There was no reason not to release her body to the mortuary. Marcella had the cremation scheduled for the next day after a private service to be held in the mortuary's chapel.

"Doctor, take a look," the medical examiner held the file open for John to read. "Right there, fifth line down, that's what did it."

"But that's a common sinus medication."

"Yes, and very useful in treating serious sinus conditions in most individuals," said the older man. "But, in this case, the young lady never had a sinus condition and the medication, taken in conjunction with a small amount of alcohol—"

"The champagne!"

"Yes, in conjunction with the champagne, it became a lethal mixture."

"Could it have been a mistake?"

"Possibly, although I'm not sure that this is the type of medication someone would arbitrarily take without needing it and it requires a doctor's prescription. I don't believe the police found any medications in her personal effects so it's not clear where the drug came from."

"Perhaps they belonged to her husband and she took one by mistake," John was trying to discount every possibility before he got to the very real possibility of premeditated murder.

Jimmy answered the telephone on the first ring. No, he didn't have a sinus problem. No, there were no prescription medicines in the house.

"What was that all about?" Marcella asked. She was waiting for Jimmy to get dressed so her driver could take them to the mortuary.

"Doctor Cunningham," replied Jimmy. "He asked about Candy's medical history."

"You said something about a sinus problem?"

"He asked if I kept any sinus medicine around the house."

Marcella's mouth felt dry.

"Here it is, the same drug. With these two it was easy enough for the ME to overlook the minute amount of a seemingly harmless legitimate drug when he was faced with the quantity of hard drugs in their bodies." The doctor held two files in his hand.

"Exact same drug?" asked John Cunningham.

"Exact same, with the same result, I might add."

"I didn't remember any indication of alcohol—"

"Oh, alcohol wasn't the catalyst with these two, doctor."

"You said the same—"

"Yes, two people, relatively healthy, no sinus history, with a common sinus medication in their bodies. And, when mixed with cocaine, it became as lethal as the mixture your poor little blonde died from."

"Coincidence?" asked John. He had his murderer in sight.

"You said these people were acquainted?"

"Yes."

"Then I wouldn't say coincidence. I think you're looking at three murders, doctor. Match the prescription to the owner and you might catch a killer. I'm filing these reports with the police."

John arrived at the mortuary just as Candy's service began. He sat two rows behind Marcella and Jimmy. The casket was closed and draped with an immense spray of yellow roses.

"She so loved yellow roses," Marcella whispered to Jimmy. She turned and glanced at John then turned to stare at the small crucifix at the back of the sanctuary.

What is he doing here, demanded the petulant child.

Just how should I know? she answered.

I don't like it, whined the child.

Neither do I, but don't you think it'd look suspicious if I demanded that he leave?

Marcella held tightly to Jimmy's arm as they watched the casket being moved from the sanctuary to the crematorium. She had no way of knowing the casket was empty and that Candy's body was still in the hospital's morgue.

Her driver took Jimmy home while she stayed until the mortuary attendants told her the cremation had been completed. In the quiet darkness of the viewing room she smiled.

Tracking A Killer

"We found it," John told Bobbi.

"Thank god," said Bobbi.

"Just one thing, what do you know about Marcella's medical history?"

"Not a lot, I mean, she has the usual, a couple allergies, nothing out of the ordinary, you know, sinus, that kind of—"

"Sinus?! You're sure?" John could feel the adrenalin rush from hearing Bobbi's words.

"That's the one thing I can remember. She took these capsules—"

"White, with a yellow band?"

"I think so, why?" asked Bobbi.

"Do you know if she carries them in her purse?"

"Yes, at least she used to. Why are you asking about her sinus medicine?" asked Bobbi.

"Because," said John. "It's the one drug that showed up in the three autopsies."

"Why would they be taking a sinus medicine?"

"They wouldn't be. They didn't need it. But our murderer knew the mix of that simple medication with alcohol or cocaine, in someone who didn't need it, would be deadly."

"So she killed Candy, Cissy and Sandra?"

"I didn't say she killed Cissy."

"But you said there were three autopsies," said Bobbi.

"I did. Cissy's was clean. Ed's wasn't."

"She killed Ed?" Bobbi whispered.

"You said he was cheating on her, that would be motive enough," said John. "Divorce would have been more logical but it was far easier just to kill him and move on."

"What about Karen?"

"She had a sinus condition as a child. Apparently she outgrew it but her prior history would have made the chemical nontoxic to her system," explained John.

"It would have killed me," said Bobbi.

"I think Marcella's smart enough to know if you all died of strokes or brain hemorrhages, someone would start putting it all together. Besides, she needed you and Chris taken out at the same time. With only one gone the other might have continued with the investigation," said John softly.

"And we couldn't both have strokes at the same time," said Bobbi.

"Not likely," replied John. "By the way, there may have been a fourth murder."

"Who?"

"Arnold Taylor."

"Arnie?"

"There doesn't seem to be any connection at this point, but based on certain wounds on the body—"

"But the police said—"

"I know what they said. Now they're taking a second look. There was an alcohol reading of point four. It's virtually impossible for someone to drink that much and remain conscious. They certainly wouldn't be able to navigate a boat out a mile long waterway, then fall overboard," said John.

"You said certain wounds?" asked Bobbi.

"Bruises to the head. During the autopsy the examiner felt they would be consistent with his falling overboard and striking his head."

"What changed their mind?" asked Bobbi.

"Saltwater in his lungs," answered John.

"But that would be consistent with a drowning," replied Bobbi.

"Yes, it would. So when none showed up in the report, I started asking questions. The doctor who did the examination said he thought it was a little strange at the time but there was so much pressure on him to finish and sign off on the case," said John.

"Pressure?"

"This one has me stumped. Some judge, and the examiner won't tell me the name, he's too scared, said close it, and so he did."

"But do you think there's a tie with Marcella?" asked Bobbi.

"I don't know."

"So what happens now?"

"I think it's time to drop the net," replied John. "Can you get a flight this evening?"

"I'll do my best."

"Call me with the details. I'll have someone meet you at the airport." John paused. "Just in case Marcella tries to get in touch with you, Joanne can tell her you've relapsed and are totally uncommunicative. Hopefully, that should hold her. If not—"

"If not, I'll be more than glad to talk to her face to face when I get there."

"I'm hoping she'll be behind bars by then."

BAITING THE TRAP

"Marcella, this is John Cunningham. I have some great news!"

"Yes, John," Marcella answered.

"It's Karen."

"Yes," Marcella drew it out as a hiss.

"She's beginning to respond. Doctor Glickman believes she may regain consciousness at any time."

Marcella held the telephone as though it was a wriggling snake. There was no way this could be happening to her.

"She bought it," said John to the stern-faced man standing next to Karen's bed.

"We'll post guards, some of our police women in nurses' uniforms, plainclothes dressed as orderlies. She won't get past us."

"Then you won't get the evidence you need," said John. He didn't like the idea of using Karen as bait, but the only way to get solid evidence against Marcella was to catch her as she made a move against Karen. He knew his phone call would draw her to Karen's hospital room.

"You're right, doctor," the detective agreed reluctantly. "But I'm still putting plenty of my people in this hospital. This lady isn't going to get harmed any more than she has already been." He looked down at the still form. "She looks like she was quite a stunning woman."

"She still is," John said softly. "She still is."

Marcella pulled the starched white uniform from the back of her closet. She bought the nurses' attire months before from a uniform shop in another city. She paid cash, not wanting her credit card to reflect the purchase. A box held new white lace-up shoes, opaque white hose, and a cap similar to those worn by the RN's at Tampa General.

She dressed hurriedly, threw her mink coat over the white uniform, thrust the cap and several hair pins into her purse. Just as she'd been prepared with the uniform, she, too, was prepared to leave no traces of her presence at the hospital. She drove the red SL coupe to Tampa Bay Shopping Mall and parked it in a handicapped space in front of Burdines. The ticket she would get would provide her with an ironclad alibi for the afternoon.

She walked over to a battered Dodge Omni and unlocked the door. She balled up the mink coat and shoved it under the front seat. Retrieving the hairpins from her purse, she pinned her unruly hair close to her scalp and positioned the cap on her head.

"Did you hear?" the young aide asked Marcella. "There's police all over the hospital!"

"What?" Marcella tried to look calm. She held a clipboard and a stolen stethoscope hung loosely from her neck. "What are you talking about?"

"The police," the girl whispered. "They're hiding to catch a killer." She looked at Marcella. "I swear! I heard some of the other nurses talking."

"You obviously don't have enough work to keep you busy!" Marcella chastised the girl. "I'll see if I can't hunt up some bedpans for you to empty to occupy your time!"

Marcella made a hasty exit from the supply room. What would police be doing in the hospital? Were they setting a trap for her? If they were, why? Or was it coincidence. Or better yet, the product of the aide's overactive imagination?

There were always police in the hospital. They routinely visited to interview people injured in accidents as well as victims of abuse and other crimes. The aide apparently needed to spice up a boring day by weaving a tale of police in hiding to catch a killer.

If, however, there was the slightest possibility the aide was telling the truth, and the police were setting a trap for her, she had the upper hand.

She had to work quickly.

Murder For One

Herbert slowly lowered the telephone to its cradle. There was no more time for delay. According to the caller, the police had evidence linking Marcella with two murders. His associates would slow down the investigation, but, too much had surfaced to be ignored.

This was one time he regretted not having control over the mayor. In the old days, one phone call would cause entire files to be lost, cases to be dropped.

He gave a deep sigh and wished again for the simplicity of the old days, where women knew their place and bullets were the accepted method of control.

Herbert called the partners together. It was time to take action before their entire cartel was exposed through Marcella's stupid actions.

Marcella did not know of Herbert's mob connection. It had been a work of fiction that she concocted for Karen on their last night together. Marcella considered Herbert to be a simpleton, an old man who bumbled through his business dealings with an inordinate amount of luck.

Herbert thought he could better control Marcella by marrying her. He had not counted on her fanatic obsessions, nor had he been even remotely aware of her murderous activities. Only after their marriage did he find out just how dangerous she could be.

The damning report produced by the cartel's investigators linked Marcella to Sandra's death, the death of reporter Arnie Turner, and the accident that killed Chris and left Bobbi in a vegetative state.

The investigators had also found evidence to link Marcella with her former husband's death. While Cissy's death was still unexplained, much pointed to the work of another person and the cartel's investigators were still probing to see what they could find.

Herbert believed Marcella's current state of mind was irrational at best and he feared the consequences should the authorities get involved if she slipped in her pursuit of silencing Bobbi or finishing the bungled job she did on Karen.

The cartel's discoveries had shocked Herbert and he was not a man who shocked easily. At first he had been outraged when the information was presented to him. How dare they go behind his back, investigate his family? And, yet, though he was the chief, the don, he had to be able to stand up to the same scrutiny as the others. Weak links had to be strengthened or eliminated. Even links at the top.

Herbert treasured his first wife. Her tragic suffering and her death by uterine cancer had taken a toll on his emotions.

Herbert knew a great deal about Sandra when he married her. He had a quick background check performed before their marriage so he knew she wasn't the innocent young girl she portrayed.

Sandra provided him with the security of a wife within the community, and his choice made him look less than intelligent to the business community. The image of the cuckold provided a good cover for him.

Herbert kept Sandra under constant scrutiny both within their home and without. Hidden cameras recorded Sandra's sexual escapades with her young maid, and the later threesomes when her father became a houseguest. The cartel distributed the resulting X-rated movies overseas under their Xanthippe label.

Sandra's cocaine use and her involvement with Greg White were monitored closely. Herbert did not like Greg but he added more credibility to the image of Herbert as the cuckold. He knew her cocaine habit would keep her absorbed in her own pursuits and away from intrusion into his personal affairs.

Herbert used Sandra as she thought she was using him. It had been an equitable relationship, one which Herbert had not been ready to end. When the autopsy indicated a lethal mixture of drugs caused her death, he had the tests re-done. The second testing, done independently of the authorities, brought out the real cause of death: a chemical of such an ambiguous nature that the medical examiner would have had no reason to test for it.

Only after surreptitious testing performed on the bodies of Arnie and Ed revealed traces of the same chemical did Herbert begin to suspect that Marcella was behind the deaths and not a rival cartel. He had been genuinely surprised. He had known Marcella for years and never believed her to be any more than a meddling social do-gooder. Life was full of surprises.

Herbert was unable to monitor Marcella's activities in Cape Cod but he was aware of a change of attitude when she returned. She was cheerful and smiling for the first time in weeks. That she was deteriorating mentally was evident by the conversations she carried on with herself in her locked bedroom.

"I'm unhappy to admit you are correct," Herbert said to the men gathered around the polished oak conference table.

"Then you will handle it?" The question came from the elderly man to his left.

"Yes."

"Forgive us, we did not mean to imply —"

"It is nothing," said Herbert as he waved a hand in the air. "We are all at risk. Thank you for bringing this to my attention."

There was a collective sigh of relief from the men around the table. They knew just how lethal Herbert could be should he be provoked. They did not wish that anger directed at them.

Herbert expected to find Marcella at home. He was angry when the servants told him she had gone shopping hours before. Shopping! The damn bitch was on the verge of ruining him and she went shopping!

He poured himself a drink. Scotch. Neat. It was his one indulgence, other than imported Cuban cigars. He looked around the large room. How he hated this sterile, modern penthouse. He would buy back his house after he took care of Marcella. No one would fault him.

He carried his drink into Marcella's study and rolled a sheet of her monogrammed notepaper into her typewriter. Using the eraser end of a pencil, he tapped out a short note. He removed the paper and slipped it into his pocket.

He walked back to the bar, pulled the crystal stopper from the baccarat decanter and took a small vial from his pocket. After emptying the vial into the decanter, he shook it to mix the poison with the brandy, and replaced the stopper. He put the decanter back on the shelf and walked from the room.

The stage was set; all he had to do was wait for his beloved wife to get her ass home. He went to his room, turned on the large-screen television, put a tape in the VCR, and relit his cigar. He smiled as the Xanthippe credit faded and the camera came in tight on Sandra's swollen clitoris.

Catching A Murderer

Bobbi's plane had been delayed in Atlanta. By the time she arrived at Tampa International she was irritated and her head ached. She found she had much less patience these past few weeks.

A handsome black man in a business suit waited at the airside gate. He approached her as she exited the runway.

"Miss Adams?" He opened his hand to display a badge.

"Yes."

"I'm to escort you to the hospital." He reached for her overnight case. "My car is this way."

"Parked in a conveniently close police zone, I suspect," quipped Bobbi.

She and her armed escort shared the joke. Bobbi was desperate to find something to laugh about.

"Looks like your suspect isn't too worried," said the detective. "She's spent the afternoon shopping, according to the officer watching her."

John took a sip of coffee and frowned.

"Coffee that bad, doc?"

"No, I was just thinking, it's not like Marcella to stay away from the hospital. She's been too intense these past few weeks to just go shopping, especially after my phone call."

Major Jack Burton nodded. "The lady seems to be most unpredictable, I'll grant you that."

"But that's just the point, most of her moves have been very predictable, that's why this shopping spree is totally out of character."

John took another sip of coffee and turned to watch as several nurses walked through the hospital's cafeteria. Bonnie, Karen's private nurse for this shift, was taking a short break. John knew there were three police guards within a hundred yards of Karen's room at any one time. Yet, he had a nagging feeling they were overlooking something.

Disguised To Kill

Marcella had no difficulty getting a syringe from the supply room on the fourth floor. The second floor, obstetrics, had been too busy for her to try. She skipped the third floor, intending to come back if she was unsuccessful on the fourth or sixth. Karen was on the fifth floor and she expected to be on that floor only as long as it took to gain access to her room and kill her.

It had been only slightly more difficult to gain access to the medicine locker on the sixth floor. Once inside, she quickly filled her syringe with a mixture of sodium pentothal and potassium chloride.

She was busily flipping pages and scribbling notes as she approached the closed door to Karen's room. She took note of the orderly scrubbing the floor and the older woman with sharp eyes who wore a candy striper's uniform. Their eyes gave them away. The police guard. She bustled past them and pushed the door open. Another sharp-eyed aide sat beside Karen's bed.

"Routine check," said Marcella crisply as she laid down the clipboard and picked up Karen's limp wrist. She looked down at her watch and moved her lips as she counted. She dropped Karen's wrist and wrote on one of the pages on her clipboard.

"Sad case, this one," she said to the aide. The woman nodded.

Marcella leaned down and placed the stethoscope on Karen's chest. She appeared to listen intently to the sounds that came through her headset. Instead, she was looking around the room, trying to figure out how to get a few minutes alone with Karen.

Karen looked down. She had been floating on a cool blue cloud and it was immensely pleasurable. It was so pleasurable that she didn't want it to end. And then she opened her eyes and what she saw confused her. She looked down into a room of stark white sheets and machinery that hummed and buzzed and beeped. There were wires and tubes attaching the machinery to the body of — no, it was not possible!

As she watched, two men walked into the room and looked down at the body — her body. One of the men walked to the window and pulled aside the heavy curtain as though he were looking for something. The other man reached for a hand — her hand — and grasped it. She could feel the man's loneliness and she wanted to call out to him, ask him to join her in the blue cloud. And then both men left the room and a woman dressed in white came in and sat down next to the bed. The woman looked solemn as she stared at the woman lying in the bed.

Karen wanted to call out but when she tried, when she said to the solemn woman, 'look up here,' there was no sound. And then the door opened again and another figure in white entered the room, held the wrist of the woman on the bed, talked in clipped sentences to the first woman.

Karen felt as though her cloud was beginning to disintegrate and that she would fall. She closed her eyes to try to bring the cloud back. She opened her eyes and looked down at the women. She was getting sensations that were foreign to her. Sensations of evil coursed through the room and up through her blue cloud.

Bobbi met John in the hospital cafeteria and he introduced her to Jack Burton, the policeman in charge of the murder investigation.

"How is she?" asked Bobbi.

"Stabilized with no change," John knew she meant Karen.

"And Marcella?"

"Shopping," replied Major Burton.

"Shopping?" Bobbi was as surprised as John had been. "That doesn't sound like Marcella."

"I've had someone watching her car for over three hours. It's parked at Tampa Bay Mall."

Bobbi turned to John. "Something's strange. You know how wound up she's been."

"That's what I've been telling the major but he assures me his people have everything well in hand."

Burton smiled. "Folks, we're securing this lady like we would some drug kingpin—"

Bobbi cut him off. "Don't patronize us! This woman is a killer! Maybe her victims are just numbers and names to you but they are people we loved!"

John reached over and patted her hand. "Come on, Bobbi, the major is taking this seriously. Don't let your nerves get you now."

"I'll get another update from my man covering her," said Major Burton as he got up from the table and motioned for the sergeant who met Bobbi at the airport to follow him. He knew these two needed some time alone. Waiting was the worst part of any case.

Marcella continued to scribble on her clipboard. There had to be a way to get this woman out of the way. There was no doubt she was another cop.

As her blue cloud disintegrated, Karen felt herself falling toward the still figure in the bed, the figure that had her features. She tried to fight but the resistance from the body in the bed was too great. As she entered the body — her body — she felt a strength she hadn't had before.

"My man says her car's still there."

John and Bobbi looked at each other.

"She won't be hard to spot when she comes out, either. My man says she's wearing a black mink coat, white shoes and white hose." Major Burton chuckled. "Today's fashions leave me a little baffled."

"Well, Marcella tries to keep up with—" John began.

"She's not a fad dresser!" exclaimed Bobbi. "And white shoes and hose aren't part of the fashion scene!" She jumped up from the table. "But they are part of a nurse's uniform!"

John's chair fell to the floor as he scrambled to his feet. "My god, she's probably in the hospital right now!"

They ran for the stairs.

Marcella looked at the still form on the floor. There had been no other option but to strike the fake aide across the head with the clipboard. Now, before the woman came to, she should have enough time to give Karen a special cocktail mixed just for her.

She reached into her pocket, drew out the syringe, removed the cap from the needle, then held it up toward the light and pushed the plunger until a thin stream of liquid squirted from the needle.

She walked around the bed and reached for the intravenous tubing that ran from the plastic bottle suspended from the metal stand to the catheter in Karen's arm. As she started to position the needle she felt a hand grip her arm.

"No, Marcella!" commanded Karen.

Marcella froze, the needle in midair. After a moment of panic, she regained her composure and attempted to pull free of Karen's grasp. But Karen held onto her arm with a strength that was solid and all Marcella could do was drop the needle and run out of the room.

The Dodge was still in the parking garage and Marcella calmed down enough to drive the car slowly from the garage. Now was not the time to get stopped for speeding or draw any more attention to herself.

She parked the car at the back corner of the shopping mall, retrieved her mink coat from under the seat, put it over her uniform, and walked quickly to the mall entrance. She made a couple quick purchases at Burdines and then, packages in hand, walked to the red Mercedes. She smiled when she saw the traffic citation on the windshield.

The three of them burst into the room at the same time. The policewoman was just getting up from the floor.

"The nurse—" said the policewoman.

"We know!" exclaimed Major Burton. He picked up the hypodermic syringe lying on the bedcovers.

John and Bobbi had moved to Karen's bedside and were staring down at her. Karen looked at them and smiled.

"Everything's okay," Karen said in a serene voice as she patted John's hand.

Tears coursed down Bobbi's cheeks as John leaned over and kissed Karen's forehead.

Home Again

Marcella pulled the Mercedes into its reserved space. Then she saw Herbert's car. Why was he home? Damnit! Nothing was going right!

She removed the hose and shoes, put on the sandals she'd purchased just a short time before, then stuffed the white hose and nurse's shoes into her shopping bag. She would dispose of them later.

She took the elevator to the penthouse.

Herbert was sitting in the living room reading a newspaper.

"Why, Herbert, what a pleasant surprise!" said Marcella as she came into the room with her packages. "Let me put these things away. I'll be right back!"

She hurried into her room, peeled off the mink coat and the white uniform, and slipped on a pair of raw silk slacks and matching blouse. She crammed the shoes, hose and uniform into a plastic bag and stashed it in the back of her clothes closet. Tomorrow she'd put them in the incinerator. Tonight she would deal with Herbert.

"She was a tall woman, about mid-fifties, I'd guess," said the policewoman. "She behaved normally. She did the routine checks. Pulse, that kind of thing. She looked and acted like she belonged here. She had dark hair, pinned up under her cap, and a strong-featured face. I'd recognize her again."

Major Burton and the policewoman were sitting at a small table in the corner of Karen's room. Huge ouquets of flowers, including yellow roses from Marcella, adorned the table.

Bobbi stood at the foot of Karen's bed. She watched as John checked Karen's pulse, blood pressure, and shined a pinpoint shaft of light into her eyes. Karen smiled up at him.

"It's a miracle," said John. "And, as a doctor, I don't believe in miracles. But, this," he pointed to the monitoring machines, "is unexplainable. For the first time since she was admitted, everything's normal."

"Of course it is, John," Karen's voice was soft and husky. "I thought it was time I came home."

TIL DEATH DO US PART

Well, you screwed that up royally!

"I'm not in a mood to listen to you."

Hey, it was a good plan. You could have taken care of that bitch once and for all.

"Well, it didn't work, so shut up!"

Marcella went into the living room.

"Did you have a good day shopping, my dear?" asked Herbert.

"Oh, so so. The shops were too crowded, and the people were pushy." She walked to the bar and reached for her decanter of brandy. "Would you like a bit of scotch?"

"Thank you, my dear, I would like that," replied Herbert. He watched as she poured herself a quarter of a snifter of brandy then reached for the crystal 'rocks' glass. He turned back to his newspaper and Marcella quickly emptied a white and yellow capsule into the glass before she poured in a couple shots of scotch.

"No rocks?" she asked.

"No rocks, neat as always, my dear," he replied.

She brought the drink to him and bent down to kiss his cheek. "You've been so good for me, you do know that?" she asked.

"And you for me," he said.

"To us," she said as she held her brandy snifter in the air.

"To us," he said.

They drained their drinks, had refills, drained them and went to their respective rooms to rest before dinner.

Herbert slipped from his room once to roll a piece of paper into Marcella's typewriter.

All's Well That Ends Well

"She's back home," Major Burton told John. "She came out of Burdines about an hour ago, loaded down with packages, and drove straight home. We'll talk with her in the morning. Unfortunately, we don't have anything to pin her to this. She was wearing surgical gloves, so there are no prints. We can't find a cabbie who remembers bringing someone in a nurse's uniform to the hospital, if that's how she got here. Our officer's description is good, and no doubt it's the same lady, but we have nothing but circumstantial evidence. The officer doing surviellance would have to testify that he saw the lady enter and leave the shopping mall during the same time frame we're alleging she was here trying to commit a murder."

"The tapes," said Bobbi. "I brought the tapes. Aren't they proof of the type of person we're dealing with?"

"Inadmissible," replied John as Major Burton nodded his head in agreement. "Done without her consent."

"But—she never would have allowed us—" sputtered Bobbi.

"That's a problem in the system," said Burton. "But it's the only system we have, and it's designed to protect all of us from the consequences of witch hunts. Maybe some do get away, but hopefully fewer innocent people are incarcerated than have been in the past."

"The law is letting killers run free!" shouted Bobbi. She turned and buried her head in John's chest and great sobs tore through her. He wrapped his arms around her and held her close. He agreed with her, but there was nothing else they could legally do. And Karen's miraculous breakthrough was uppermost in his mind.

"SOCIETY MURDER-SUICIDE" — It was the lead story on the six o'clock news, occupied the top half of the front page of the local newspaper the next morning, and, by the next day, was old news.

Marcella and Herbert had not appeared for dinner the evening before, a fact that didn't upset their maid. Sporadically they chose to ignore meals without informing the servants.

When neither appeared for breakfast the next morning, the servants remained unperturbed. All the less work for them to do.

Major Burton's detectives arrived at the penthouse apartment mid-morning. Mary went to Marcella's room to announce their arrival and discovered her body. She ran screaming from the room. The detectives then discovered Herbert's body in his room. Autopsies would later confirm traces of sinus medication in Herbert's body, poison in Marcella's.

A search of the apartment turned up the plastic bag with the nurse's uniform as well as a short note in Marcella's typewriter: "It's all been too much. Please forgive me. m." It was clear, Marcella had murdered Herbert and then taken her own life after her botched attempt on Karen.

Case closed.

Among The Living

"I can't believe it's over," Bobbi said to John. He called her after he received a call from Burton with the news. They met for coffee in the hospital cafeteria.

"I know. It's been such a drain on our emotions that ending like this seems anticlimactic," he said.

"You're going to dislike me for this, but I wanted her to suffer."

"Believe me; your feelings aren't unusual for what she put you through. My god, as far as we know, she killed Chris, or at least arranged for it to be done. And your newspaper friend. That's enough reason for you to feel like you do."

"I just think she got off too easy," said Bobbi.

"I do too," said John. "I would've enjoyed seeing her lying in a hospital bed, paralyzed, with tubes running into her body, feeling the pain that Karen did and not being able to do anything to stop it. Believe me, nothing would have pleased me more, and it's very unprofessional for me to wish that on anyone."

"But Karen—"

"Right. I'd like adequate revenge for what was done to Karen and yet she's better than she was and apparently her recovery was triggered by Marcella's attack."

"It's amazing," said Bobbi. "Look close enough and something good came from that horrible encounter."

"Good? I'd call it damn miraculous!"

"You're right," said Bobbi. "It'll take some time, I suppose, to get over the anger. But, right now, I have plenty of time. And you, John, what do you do now?"

"First, there's a certain lady I've got to get back on her feet. And then, I'm going to ask her to be my wife."

"Ummmmm."

"I've come to realize how short and how precious life really is. Even being a doctor, treating patients, having some die, doesn't prepare you for the personal pain of seeing someone you love just hours or minutes away from dying. I thought I was immune to that after my first wife died. No, this time I won't hesitate to tell Karen how I feel and I'll do everything in my power to get her to marry me."

"Just hearing you talk makes me feel good," said Bobbi. "And, I don't think you're going to have to struggle all that hard with Karen despite her vow to never love someone enough to marry them. Instinct tells me that she loves you very much. I saw the way she looked at you when she came out of her coma."

"That's what I'm counting on."

Happily Ever After

A full year passed.

John was a constant companion during Karen's recovery and by the time he got up the courage to propose, she had the courage to accept.

Bobbi, meanwhile, fell in love with the cardiologist who had been overseeing her case. In time, their relationship moved from doctor and patient to lovers.

The two couples exchanged vows in a double candlelight ceremony then flew to a posh St. Thomas resort. Four days later, Bobbi and her new husband left to explore the Amazon jungle. Five days later, Karen and John flew to Paris to begin a month long European honeymoon.

www.ingramcontent.com/pod-product-compliance
Lightning Source LLC
Chambersburg PA
CBHW050023180626
46810CB00002B/549